RED
BRICKS

A novel by
Anne Muccino

Rocket Science Press
SHIPWRECKT BOOKS PUBLISHING COMPANY

IN
DIE

Minnesota

Front cover desert panorama by Lauren Fountain.
Red bricks from a photo by Dan Coffey.
Cover and interior design by Shipwreckt Books

To Susan, Mary, Carol and Margie, who shaped me in ways I am still discovering.
And to Daniel and Jack, who I've had the privilege of shaping, and who remain my bricks.

1.

I was born in the brumal season in the time of the otter when the ground breathed snow and ice and earth's awakening was not yet contemplated by the dormant clay, and what saved me in that difficult breaching was the power of my water totem. So my *abuelita* says. For it is she who examined the placenta then washed the umbilical cord and buried it in the fields, not in the corner of the house where the feet of women are rooted. Like Moses who struck the rock twice, she doubted the strength of my place in this world and sought to lift it where rain reaches and my totem can breathe. It is from this, my mother says, my rebellion comes. It is why in my younger years she found me standing outside the house in the nakedness of a storm, drinking in its music. And like Moses, my grandmother was punished for her sins by not living long enough to see the fruits of her labor ripen. There is no going back and undoing what is stone, and I thank her every day.

I have lived in Las Cruces, New Mexico for as long as I can remember, and longer even before that. My dreams take me to these same streets, this same place, but in these dreams I am dressed in pants with a vaquero's hat that sits worn on my head and my name is Lucas. I am not so tall, but taller than most, and the dream ends the same each time in the streets of Las Cruces where I am shot dead with a bullet to the heart and then I have no further memories of that life. Because I am dead.

Here my name is Dalia. My mother is a Nahua half-blood and married my white father two years before I arrived. My eyes are the dusky green of tortoise shell and my hair is the color of iron rusted in salt water and when the boys come, they ask to touch it to see if the fire is hot on their hands. We live on my father's ranch in a stucco house painted white with a red tiled roof now the shade of salmon where the word *Paraíso* is lettered in the wood that shadows the entrance. Here I am not encouraged to wear pants and my father says I must marry. My 15th birthday approaches in the spring, and at that time I will be prepared in the ways of women so that I will not embarrass my family or my future husband. My father says that he did not make these rules, that these rules existed even before he was born and that he does not have the power to change them. I see in my mother's eyes that she does not agree, that she once stood where I am now and longed for the freedoms I desire, yet she will not oppose my father. And when I say *'nantli*, you must help me,' she turns away and stares through the window to the south where her people come from, and I know that her mind is set. In this way I am alone.

It is a hard thing, to hate one's father, the man who taught me to ride, the man who loves my mother, the one whose seed I spilled from. The laws of nature forbid it and I feel I am forever travelling breathless up the backward slope of a mountain with only small hope to hold. Moments I think it impossible to hate him, moments I know it is impossible not to. This is why I must believe in God. Because I pray every day for a miracle to change my father's heart. And because He has bent down to kiss the earth with the spirits of its beasts, knowing that I will live forever if I can always feel the girth of a horse between my legs. That is the Lucas in me.

2.

They carried them from the well to lay at the foot of his grave, hoping thieves wouldn't steal them in the night. Dusty red adobe bricks. Baked in the heat of the New Mexico sun, the deep color of a roan quarter horse, brushed 'til its sides shined.

Granddad would have liked that, the simplicity of a man's mark in the world boiled down to a heap of red bricks. It said something about him. About his tenacity, his slow nurturing patience that allowed him to go forward while others stalled. Something a carved piece of granite couldn't say. He never tired of getting his hands wet in the muck of earth and water, and their rooted solidness bore him on when the outside world wore him down. He was humbled by the land and the way it sang to him when his hands heaved the clay from the sweltering ground, shaping his future brick by brick, waiting for them to dry in the oppressive desert heat.

JT loved that old man.

They stood at the rim of the hole they dug, but not too close. Yesterday's rain made the ground soggy and weak under their feet. The unearthed dirt stank of pitch and darkness and of things that never see light. Nine feet of hole severs you so completely from a loved one that you almost ache to crawl into the hole with them. *Almost.* At the same time truth motions you to step forward in line because you're that much closer to the grave yourself. Joke's on you. Granddad would have laughed at that. Would have said there was no getting around it. If you worry about it, you die. If you don't worry about it, you die. What's the point? It's what you did in the time before the dying that mattered.

Harlan's roughed hands curled the brim of his hat. JT knew he wanted to say something more than the obligatory prayers. Something important that would last and cause them to pause when they thought back on this day. But Pa hollered at them to "hurry it up" and "we ain't got all day," and Harlan can't think well when he's under that kind of pressure. When Pa turned to go, Harlan cleared the tightness in his throat and spoke.

"You stay dead, ol' man."

That made Pa laugh, a little "heh heh" sound they weren't expecting. Both boys fixed him with a hard look to see if he'd been drinking.

Funny wasn't in the way Harlan meant it—JT knew that. His brother loved Granddad as much as he did, maybe more. It was just Harlan's way of telling him to rest easy, that there was no sin in wanting to escape this life. They understood the misery of sitting in a wheelchair day after day, bearing witness to the ruin and neglect overrunning the homestead he sunk his heart into, watching all he worked for collapse. Watching Pa abandon the land and indulge himself, spending money on god knows what. Harland and JT knew what, but they weren't to say it out loud. No man should have to tolerate suffering like that just because they've outlived the use of their legs. That last year Granddad was already living dead.

"And whatcha bring those bricks out from the well for? They don't belong here." Before they could stop him, Pa picked one up and dropped it in the grave. A dry thud echoed as brick thumped the pine coffin and lay still. JT looked to Harlan and saw the muscles in his jaw working and the thin line that was now his mouth. Then Pa looked up at the sky and told them to move along, those were rain clouds setting in and wouldn't that just be the shits if they got caught in the middle of a bucket down with a half-dug grave. "I'll be waiting in the truck," he said.

JT hated that old man.

Harlan put his hat back on and glared at Pa's back, then picked up two spades and threw one to his brother. They began to shovel the unearthed dirt over the coffin. The hollow sound of dirt hitting wood undid JT some, and he was glad when they finally reached the point where dirt was hitting dirt. This was his second grave digging. The first was Ma's when JT was ten, a sound he hated even more then.

When they got back to the house, Pa told them to listen up so they took seats at the table while he reached for the whiskey bottle. He brought down three glasses from the shelf.

"You boys gonna hear about this sooner or later, so I might as well tell you now." He poured the whisky into one of the glasses and drank it down. Then he refilled the glass and the others next to it. "I'm selling the ranch."

They stared through him like he was a ghost. He lifted the whiskey to his lips a second time and threw it back.

"You can't do that," Harlan said.

"Shut up." Pa slapped the glass down on the table, making the drink in the other two jump. Then he leaned across the table towards Harlan. "Last time I needed to check with you, boy, about what I can and cannot do, was *never*."

A sudden stillness entered the room and JT felt the electricity between them spark like a live wire being tapped. It didn't take much to set Pa on edge, especially after a day of drinking, and they knew the danger in offering up any kind of resistance. He'd seen Pa bully Harlan before. But this was different. There was a growing up to Harlan that JT hadn't noticed, and he could tell his brother wasn't backing down. He could see it in the way Harlan's elbows dug deep into the table, and the naked heat he directed at Pa. It wasn't long before he heard the scrape of Harlan's chair as it pushed back and he made to stand.

"It ain't your land to sell," Harlan said. "He wanted it to stay with us."

No one spoke.

Then suddenly Pa laughed, only this time it was a raucous laugh that shook his throat. He put the whiskey bottle to his lips and took a swig, wiping his mouth with the back of his hand, the smile disappearing from his face. From his jeans he pulled a pocketknife and picked up an apple from the basket on the floor.

"You'll always be the fool, son," he said, narrowing his eyes at Harlan. "I don't know what that ol' man told you, don't care. This ranch is mine and there ain't a damn thing you can do about it." The knife cut a slit deep into the apple's skin. He broke off a chunk and stuffed it in his mouth, licking the juice off the blade, all the while keeping his eyes on Harlan. "Set yourself down."

There was something familiar to JT about the temperature rising in a room that came from growing up with it all his life. When he was young he couldn't ignore the swell of adrenaline dribbling into his veins that interrupted the living of an ordinary life. It promised the spark of something new. But that changed the night Pa's drinking got out of control and Ma got hurt, and they all came to realize how dangerous living in a pressure cooker can be. The truth was they were all sitting atop a bundle of dynamite with Pa holding the matches. From that night forward a cold fear moved with them throughout the house, throughout their lives, making the tiniest change in routine a threat. It changed the way JT saw the world, and he got to trembling inside each time he felt it enter the house.

The day she got hurt was the day Granddad came back to life. He came out of his wheelchair and stood between them, shaking with such fury that the finger he pointed at Pa was wobbling. Little bubbles of spit formed in the corners of his mouth. "If you ever ..." he said, his finger folding back into his hand to make a fist. It was scary seeing the veins in his forehead throb. "If you ever," he repeated, "touch her again ..." then his words trailed off and stopped, like he wasn't sure what came next. His eyes swept the room and took in Ma on the floor bleeding and Harlan at ten years old kneeling beside her, and JT eight years young in his PJ's trembling.

"I'll *kill* you." He said these words in a low voice that had lost its roar but none of its promise. Pa didn't speak. They stared at each other while time stood still. Then Pa walked away, the screen door slamming behind him. The world was silent with the sound of Ma crying.

Only this time it wasn't Granddad, it was Harlan, and JT knew with absolute certainty that Pa wasn't walking away. Inside he felt the buildup of the tremble threatening to climb out of him all day. He rose to his feet on shaky legs, not certain which way the dynamite was going to pitch, and what he was supposed to do. And just when he thought all hell would break loose, the world lit up outside like it was daybreak and a roaring boom ripped the sky. In the next instant the pounding of thunder hammered the roof of the house like a stampede of horses. The storm broke free.

"Shit," Pa said. "Those calves are loose in the south pasture. Gotta get 'em before they drown."

There was no room for arguing. He was right, those calves had to be found. But JT could see reluctance in Harlan's face. It was hard to surrender courage when it's just gaining breath—you never know when you're going to find it again. A weariness came over his brother as Harlan reached for his hat, and JT knew the fight had gone out of the room. At least for now.

"JT, run out and turn those horses loose," Pa said. "If lighting hits the barn, they can't be hemmed in."

Harlan shook his head. "No way a truck will make it down the embankment in this rain without sinking in the muck. Going to have to saddle up. Best you take care of the horses in the barn, old man, and me and JT will collect the calves."

Pa's back straightened and his eyes went cold. "I was born on a horse, boy," he said, "if there's any saddling up, I'll be part of it."

JT looked to his brother, his eyes begging Harlan to step down.

"I can handle the horses," JT said.

"I know you can," Harlan said.

"Then whatcha waitin' for?" Pa said.

Harlan ignored Pa and looked straight at JT. "You come along after you loose the horses, hear? And stay clear of the creek. It'll be swollen. Don't take no chances, you hear?"

"I hear."

"If one of those calves go in, you let it go, you hear?"

JT nodded.

"Don't be stupid."

"I won't."

"Stop yapping and get to it then," Pa said.

Those were the last words JT ever heard him speak.

A wide arc of lightning passed overhead as JT made his way to the barn, and it wasn't but two seconds before he heard the clap of thunder ride up behind it. He heard the whinnying of the horses and their hooves tap-tapping the ground as the thunder cracked. He opened the barn doors wide and stepped in, the dark musk of the horse muddied stalls pushing against him, the rain in the air making it sweeter. It brought him back to Granddad and how the man craved leaning into that smell every chance he got. He said it gave consequence to his life and reminded him every day that horses were a gift from heaven. Pa said the stink of livestock always brought him back to the slaughterhouses his family sent him to work in when he was a boy spending ten hours a day shin-deep in blood.

JT opened the first three stalls and the horses bolted, kicking dust as they broke. They didn't need his permission. In the next two stalls he had to do some persuading. He coaxed the black bay and the mare out with help from the thunder that rained down hard again, so ear-splitting he saw white. When he swung open the last stall, JT could tell Ruby was staying put. She had backed into a corner of the stall and was shivering from head to toe. "Come on, baby," he whispered trying to sweet talk her into moving, but her eyes were wide like they'd been stretched flat against a sharp blade. Her breathing was grunted and heavy, and he knew she was in a bad place. He'd have to ride her out. JT grabbed her halter off the hook and came close, holding out his hand so she could smell it, all the while her snorting and stamping with those wide eyes. Just as he slipped it over her head she jerked away, but he managed to grab hold of her mane. As he swung himself up onto the sweatiness of her back, a spool of thunder rolled over the roof again and he felt himself lift into the air as she reared and flew forward like a coyote on fire. They crashed out of the stall and he thought for sure he was going to lose his grip. But the rhythm of her gait was like breathing to him, and instead of fighting he gave into it. They soared out into the husk of the storm, the unexpected relief of rain pelting their heads and draining their thirst. The air was thick with water, and there was no seeing through it.

The darkness of the downpour made JT lose his bearings and he was helpless to steer her in any one direction. He called out to her above the rain, above the thunder and the lightning but if she heard him, she refused to listen. Both of them soaked to the bone and still she kept going. He pulled up hard on the halter, shifting his weight over her haunches, bearing down to signal her to stop, but she refused. Lightning charged and he could make out the outline of the old sycamore tree. That's when he knew they were headed towards the creek. JT knew the creek would be swollen. He couldn't let her take him down into the muddy water where they'd both surely drown.

"Whoa," he yelled about a dozen times but she kept on. And just when he'd made the decision to surrender, to let go and take his chances hitting the ground, a bolt of lightning lit up the night and she came to a dead halt. For a moment JT thought she had been struck, the way her hooves fastened to the ground and her body went rigid. He was re-centering his weight when another zigzag of electricity ignited the sky, and that's when he saw them.

Pa stood in the distance, his arm across his forehead trying to ward off the blow. Next to him must have been Harlan, his raised arm coming down towards Pa with something solid; something that squared in his hand. A rock, no—a *brick*. Then the lightning blew out and there was only darkness and rain until he and Ruby took in the thunder and she reared. He felt himself tumbling. He didn't remember meeting the ground. A loud buzzing in his ears cancelled out everything. Everything except the splash of water and Ruby's whinny as she disappeared into the creek. Then the world disappeared.

JT woke up two days later and knew Pa was dead. He knew this because sometime during those forty-eight hours Pa had passed through his dreams—sat on the rim of them begging JT to make the journey over to where he was sitting. Holding out a piece of red licorice in his hand. JT could see the black clouds gathering behind Pa, and something in the way they knew his father scared him. It was the kind of dream that makes you wake up reaching for the light and feeling drained out of yourself, relieved you were on solid ground. Only he couldn't wake up. Not then. And when he finally did open his eyes, every fiber in his body was alive with the knowledge that he came just that close to never waking up again.

He didn't see Harlan in his dreams, so it hit him hard when they told him he was gone.

"What do you mean, gone?"

They stared him down, studying his face, trying to read something that wasn't there, trying to decide if they were reading it right.

"He's dead, JT."

At that moment the floor at the pit of his stomach gave way and he felt hollow, less than a whole person. Like he was holding something in his hand and it just vanished. *Poof.* He could almost hear the word inside his head, helping him to understand that part of him just broke. A small hiccup in the heart's rhythm that stifled his breathing, just for a second, when he tried to stop time and realized he couldn't.

Everything the sheriff's men said after that felt tired and far away. How they found Pa sprawled out on the granite ledge overlooking the river, a few yards from the sycamore, his skull caved in. They assumed he lost his footing and fell, hitting his head on the rock. How they found Harlan on the south side of the creek in the shallow reeds lining the riverbed, Ruby's halter tangled in his arms. It looked like he drowned trying to save her, but they didn't know for sure. They tracked where his horse's hooves went in from the north of the river. That didn't sound right, given what JT saw, but he didn't say.

He told them what he remembered. How the storm got out from under them, and how Pa and Harlan went to rescue the calves, how he freed the horses and fell from Ruby, and how everything went black after that. He left out the part about the raised brick, figuring whatever he thought he saw in the lightning of a rain-cussed sky was no more reliable than his dream vision of Pa beckoning him towards hell.

"What?" they asked.

"Nothing."

"You got somethin' more to say, say it."

"I got nothin'."

"You sure?"

And just when he thought they were never going to let up, the tall one in the back with the sideburns told them to lay off. The boy had just lost his whole goddamn family for chrissake.

B y the time the ranch sold, the snow had set down on the ground in small pockets of white gauze, so delicate looking you wanted to scoop them up with a butterfly net. The sale took longer than expected because of the conditions he laid down. The graves were not to be disturbed. JT had bricked a low wall around the perimeter of the plot where they were buried, and it now looked a proper cemetery. Whether the new owners would honor those conditions he had no idea, but he set it down in writing, and in his head it was done. He buried Pa out in the south acre underneath the old sycamore tree. A lot of folks thought that was disrespectful, not including him with the family, but those who knew Pa weren't surprised. It was JT's business and he got to thinking he'd sleep easier if he knew the rest of them weren't spending eternity lying next to the devil.

The money from the sale of the ranch paid off his father's debts and left JT with a small pocket full of cash. He wasn't sorry he sold it. He didn't want to be living with the ghosts of his past the rest of his life. He knew Granddad would want him to live his own dreams and not get wrapped up in holding a place for his. He planned to head west towards California where he heard the land was fertile and its beauty something to behold. He couldn't allow himself to think about Harlan yet and let the finality of his being gone sink in. It might open a floodgate he couldn't dam back up, and it scared him. Afraid it would drag him under and if that happened there was nothing and nobody that could get him up again. Truth was, he recognized death calling when he heard it and knew he had to move along or get swallowed up in grief. Laying down ain't in the Swain boys. Harlan taught him that.

JT walked Ruby out of the stall and stopped to tighten the cinch. He swung up into the saddle and nickered her forward, looking towards the west, feeling the weight of uncertainty on his shoulders. Yes, Ruby survived the storm. If it was Harlan's doing, he'd never know. It seemed a whole lot of foolishness to risk your life over a horse and Harlan would have known that. JT kept wondering if during those two days there was a small part of him that passed through Harlan's world while he was getting back to his own, but he couldn't bring it forward in his mind. He hoped it'll come back to him, like a slow memory that blows out of the dust, and you have to stop to remember whether it really happened or you dreamt it, or both. His mind hadn't summoned it yet, but he had time. And that was a good thing.

3.

He was four days out when he realized he was being followed. He dropped off the trail, then doubled back to take measure of the tracks and was surprised to see they were animal. He wasn't expecting that. They were too big for wolf, or at least he hoped so. Alone in wolf territory carried its own mess of worries. When the night lays down a dankness to the air and dark wraps its arms tight across your chest, that's when the wolves on the plains come alive. They howl in the darkness, talking with each other, telling themselves things only their ears are meant to hear, wanting him to know that it is by their good grace he's laying claim to a piece of their night.

On the third day JT spotted the cur. It tracked him at a safe distance, far enough back to mask its scent from Ruby, but close enough to keep him in sight. He got down off the horse, then pulled his rifle from the saddle and sighted the stray along the barrel. His finger eased onto the trigger and he felt the drag of the hammer as he drew back and took aim. When he jerked the muzzle away to fire at the rocks, the animal skittered, and he knew by the way it moved it wasn't no wolf. Some kind of mongrel or half-breed set out in the middle of nowhere by misfortunate circumstances. That's when it occurred to him that he and this animal had something in common. He climbed back into the saddle and rode on. Even behind him at 100 yards, he could feel the cur's breath on his neck. And it felt good.

When dusk settled JT stopped for the night and made camp in a shaded-up pine grove beside a stream. He walked Ruby out into the water and loosened the cinch, then stood there while she drank, staring at the sky. Few things in this world are as beautiful as the closing in of nightfall when the orange ball goes down and sends a spray of red and gold across the horizon and you look and look but can't see where it ends and secretly you hope it never ends because that gives strength to the idea that life never ends. Granddad told him that truth is like that—it hangs on this earth a mighty long time—and warned him to be careful with what he made of it. Truth was the one thing that didn't need explaining, and not to bother hiding from it because it would always find you and stare you down. Even when the deep dark seediness of it was painful to undress. The pain was in trying to hold onto a memory when you knew it was a lie, and the longer it set, the uglier it looked. JT's truth was that he was glad Pa was dead, even though he knew it was an unnatural thing to feel. But thinking it out loud in his head was a release, freeing him from the tether that roped him to the past. What Granddad didn't tell JT was that the truth carried with it a weariness that sobered one to the failures in their life. And the grim realization that without the assholes of the world, none of us would be able to recognize the good guys, and that was a terrible thought because that's saying one can't be had without the other. And if that was so, the world would never free itself of hell on earth.

After settling Ruby, JT skinned the rabbit he caught at the shallow creek bed earlier in the day, spitted it and laid it over the fire to cook. The snapping and sizzling smell of roasted meat brought the stray to the edge of the camp, hunger driving it forward, fear keeping it checked. Ruby picked up its scent and whinnied, letting JT know it was close.

He spoke in a soft voice, not saying anything of particular importance, still keeping his eyes focused on the fire. A rabid animal would meander into camp without fear and this one was plenty filled with it, but he kept his pistol nearby all the same. He turned the spit, all the while talking smooth, keeping his voice friendly and low without looking in its direction. It hung back in the shadows but he knew it was hungry. If it wanted something from him, he needed something from it. And that was to come just that much closer. One step and then another. He turned towards the animal and it bolted, retreating into the darkness. He "here boy'd" it, holding the piece of rabbit in his hand, showing it, letting the stray smell it. The animal stepped forward, then back, then forward again. Only its forefeet were exposed in the fire's light. They were the color of wet sand, and he watched as drops of saliva dampened the dirt at the tips of them. JT called it forward, but it wouldn't come. It retreated into dark, leaving behind the stained wetness on the ground. Not many hungry dogs would pass up a meal when they were starving, unless the amount of mistrust pent up in their minds far outweighed their need to breathe. He knew what that felt like. His hand swung and threw the meat. The animal skittered, but after a while he heard grunts in the dark as it swallowed the pieces whole. Then silence.

The next morning a cold rain fell and the air turned misty and wet. The fire had blown out long ago, in that time before night makes peace with dawn, and there was no movement of any kind, except a low undulating wind crisscrossing the plains. He was alone.

The next five days were uneventful, save for the downpours that lengthened his days, the rain soaking him clear down through his boots, whitewashing the land clean. The smell of earth and the sense of newness that washed over the plains had an odd quality to it, and he stopped and sat Ruby for a few minutes to savor the feeling. Then he pressed his heels against the horse's ribs and moved on. He kept close to the trail, but off the beaten track, remembering he was a guest in this territory and treating it as such. He made his way past Tucumcari, then stopped in Santa Rosa just long enough to dry out and get himself a meal. From there he headed to the outskirts of Carrizozo and stopped at a cantina for supper where he declined the special of the day, carne de coyote tacos, and ate chicken tacos instead, wrapped in greasy brown paper that smelled of coyote.

Now and then JT felt the cur behind him. Sometimes it was in the way Ruby reached behind and snuffed, sometimes it was in the way the gravel shifted, or when a sixth sense dictated he was not alone. Each night they broke bread together, and although the animal had not wholly given over to trusting him, they were making progress. When JT threw the cur its dinner two nights prior, it stayed put to receive it. And last night the animal ventured farther out into the fire light. JT got his first good look at how long she had been scavenging.

The mongrel was a rawboned thing, and he had no doubt if he were to rub his hands along her ribcage he would feel the bones protruding against her skin. The cartilage in her left ear was broke and the flap hung limply to the side, the symmetry of her face cockeyed. A deep gash raked across her muzzle had left an ugly scar that trailed off along the jaw line. Her fur was ragged and stained with red mud, showing signs of mange at the hind quarters, and he saw that when she shifted, she favored her right back foreleg. Her coat was spattered white with large patches of umber, bringing to mind the barred owl they caught sight of last summer on the ranch. Pa brought it down with a six shooter just for sport, and he and Harlan secretly cursed him for it. They could still hear its mate calling vainly from its roost, *who-cooks-for-you, who-cooks-for-you-all*, not yet contemplating the deafened silence.

JT watched the animal lie down, but when he turned towards her, she stood and squared off. Her eyes were the one thing seemingly untouched by the ravages of the wilderness, deep set and dark almond in color. They glowed with such tenacity and grit it was hard to reconcile them with the disfigured animal. When he looked into those eyes he realized his stake in this was bigger than he had bargained for, that he needed this more than he wanted it, and more than he had led himself to believe. It was just going to take more time. Time was something he was heavy with.

She trusted him enough to come out into the light and accept the nourishment he offered up daily. He spoke softly to her each night, telling her some of the truth he still held inside himself and hadn't spoken out loud to anyone. He talked about Harlan and how much he missed him and how wishing for him was not going to bring him back, no how. That he was waiting for some kind of glimpse of him. He couldn't believe his brother would ever totally abandon him, even in death. She couldn't make sense of his words, but he hoped she understood the timbre of his voice to soothe, not threaten. She stayed her distance and then eventually laid down again, her unyielding eyes aflame in the blue black of the fire.

JT closed his eyes and dreamt of wild dogs and wolves, and of standing in the dark on the precipice of a steep bluff, dropping a lantern into its mouth and watching the light die out as it descended into the bowl and then surrounded by darkness once more.

When he awoke during the early dawn, the air was thick with dew, the fire out. And he was alone.

The next day he rode through a low mountain range and found himself outside of the city of Alamogordo, bordered on one side by an escarpment that rimmed the plateau. He made camp that night in the bank of an arroyo and made a meal out of a pair of quail that surprised him by scaring out of the brush as he came alongside them. He brought them down within a yard of each other and after the feathers were plucked there was little meat to be had, but he figured enough for a meal and some scraps. He set a pot of beans over the fire and mixed in the quail meat, the sweet nutty flavor rising into the air. As he bent to stir the stew, a movement to his left made him reach for his rifle. A man stood ten feet from him. When the stranger took sight of the gun, he raised his hands.

"Easy there hombre," the man said, drawing the words out. "I'm one of the good guys."

JT kept the rifle trained on his chest, not trusting the idiocy of someone sneaking up on a person the way he did. He took in the bruised clothes that smelled strong of horse and sweat, the creased grease lines along its threads, the hair matted under his hat. An unshaven growth covered his chin; and holstered in his belt a Colt revolver. The man turned and spat, and JT followed its trajectory. His jaw tightened when he noticed the spurs on the stranger's boots.

"Get yourself killed coming up on a person like that," JT said.

"Didn't mean to surprise you."

"What did you mean?"

"I should have called out."

"Why didn't you?"

"Wasn't thinking, that's all."

"Get yourself killed not thinking."

"Are we back to that again?"

JT waited.

The rider raised his shoulders and gestured helplessly with his hands. "Truth is, I didn't know I was planning to stop 'til the very last. The smell of whatever you're cooking convinced me," the man said. They eyed each other a few moments longer, then JT lowered the rifle and motioned for him to sit.

From the pot JT spooned himself a plate, then filled the ladle full and handed it to the stranger. The man supped from the spoon and tore into the flesh of the quail, sucking the bones clean, the grime under his fingernails deep and black. JT ate, keeping scraps on his plate to throw to the stray.

"Finished?" the man asked, eyeing JT's plate.

"No."

The man licked the ladle clean. "Where you headed?" he said.

"West."

"Just west?"

"Just west."

"Look, we got off on the wrong foot here. I smelled the stew you was cooking, that's all. Didn't mean to startle you none. Name's Roy." The man held out his hand. JT made no move towards it.

"JT."

"That stand for something?"

"Just JT."

"Glad to meet you JT." Roy withdrew his hand and touched the brim of his hat. "A man gets lonely out here without company."

The fire crackled. Wind trapped in the low swale of the grasslands fashioned a whistling sound that blew over and around the camp.

"Where you headed?" Roy said.

"I thought we covered that."

"Did we?"

"You sure ask a lot of questions."

"Do I?"

"I just said you did."

"Just trying to make conversation."

JT realized he was nursing a grudge against the man. His coming up out of the night spooked him.

"Where you headed?" JT asked.

"Mexico."

"You plan to get there on foot?"

"My horse is alongside yours down yonder."

"Mexico is a pretty big place."

The man laughed. "Don't I know it. I'm looking to cross the border at Juárez."

"Why Juárez?"

"I've been there before." Roy said. "And you?"

"I'm headed to California."

"You've got a ways to go."

"Don't I know it."

They both laughed.

"Where's home?" Roy asked.

"Clayton."

Roy nodded. "Clayton's a pretty place."

JT doubted the man had ever been to Clayton and was only working at being polite, but he nodded just the same. Then everything after that happened real fast. Roy stood and drew his gun. Before JT could stop him, he pulled back on the hammer and fired three times into the bush.

"Goddamn scavengers," Roy said.

JT came headlong at Roy, knocking the gun from his hand and kicking it across the dirt. "What the hell?" Roy said.

JT's hands curled into fists. "You best leave."

"It's just a mangy cur. Maybe even rabid."

"It ain't rabid."

"Is that your animal?"

"No."

"What the hell you gettin' so fired up about?"

"Like I said. You best leave."

Roy's mouth opened to speak, then closed again. He re-holstered his gun and stared at JT, then shook his head. "Adios."

JT watched him go. He strained to hear the horse's hooves set off on the hardness of the ground, the sound gradually getting faint. Then he walked to the bush. Stretched out in mock surrender lay the stray, unmoving, her tongue stretched out. Blood spilled at the corners of her mouth. He took off his hat and laid it on the ground. With the heels of his hands he rubbed his eyes that burned hot to the very back of his skull. Everything he touched turned to shit.

4.

He rode into Mesilla, New Mexico on a day that was hot, gritty, and tasted a whole lot like vinegar. The harsh acidy clank of wagon wheels grinding to a stop in the dust, the metal bits in the horses' mouths as cowboys hitched them to the posts, the chains on their spurs clinking alongside their boots. The undertaker hollering to the barber, "Shit, no rain in the last two weeks and the ground is hard as stone." A small breeze blew strands of dust across the road and then it was gone, leaving behind a boiled-down sweat to the air that smelled of blackened tortillas. He walked the horse into town.

The street was deserted, the hottest part of the day making its rounds. An old Mexican stood by the side of the road, selling hand-woven baskets from a supply he pulled off a tumbledown cart. His left eye was pinched shut, leaving a furrowed slit where his eye should have been. The other had a thick milky quality to it and from it came no light. The man's straw hat was round and lay squat on his graying hair, sheltering his leathered face from the sun.

"¿Canastas?" He held up a basket.

"No, gracias. ¿Qué dia es?"

"¿Canastas? ¿Le gustaría una canasta? "

"¿Cuanto?"

"Un peso."

JT fished in his pocket and pulled out a coin that he handed down to the Mexican. The blind man felt along his arm, took the peso from his hand, and placed in his palm a small purple and yellow basket the size of a small cat.

"Gracias señor. Gracias." The man nodded in the air.

"Se toma," JT said, handing the basket back. But the Mexican shook his head.

"¿Qué dia es?" JT asked.

The old man looked towards his voice with a blank expression, his face raked with many lines. "Miercoles."

"No. Perdon. ¿Cual es la fecha?"

"El ocho de Mayo."

A trio of Mexican boys passed by in the street. They jeered at the old man. "One-eye," they taunted in Spanish, booing and hissing in his direction. The old man ignored them.

"Gracias. ¿Donde esta…" JT realized he didn't know the Spanish word for blacksmith. "Mi caballo, necesita…" he searched for the right word. "Mi caballo necesita *zapatos*." The old man nodded and rested his hand on Ruby's muzzle, then followed it down the forearm to the fetlock, gently tapping on it. Ruby shifted her weight and he lifted up her foot. He felt along the rail of her hoof, crumbling the dirt in his hand, nodding his head as he did so.

"El herrero se encuentra al final de la calle, en frente del hotel."

In front of the hotel. That sounded good. A real bed and a bath to rinse off the grime and stink of the past three weeks.

"Gracias señor." JT touched his thumb to the brim of his hat before remembering the man was blind.

Sí, sí," the old man said.

JT moved Ruby forward and gently placed the purple yellow basket on top of the cart, then rode up the street toward the hotel. As he passed the boys, his saddlebag caught the tall one in the back and knocked him down.

A loud smack thudded as he hit the ground and dust blew up around him. JT turned his head back in the boy's direction.

"Lo siento, hijo. Un accidente."

The boy scowled. Behind him, the old Mexican smiled.

The smithy accepted payment for the shoeing and JT settled Ruby at the livery stables. He crossed the road to the Mesilla Hotel and climbed its broad steps, the boards creaking under his weight. The hotel was an aged, two-storied tenement house whose dilapidated sign swung low on hooks bored into splintered wood. Drawn in hand-lettered print on the bottom of the sign was the town's population recorded at 103. A line had been drawn through the number and 101 written below it. A gentleman stepped out of the hotel carrying a broom. "Howdy." He held the screen door open.

"Howdy." The screen door slammed shut behind JT. He turned to watch the gentleman start at one end of the weathered veranda, sweeping the dirt from the edge, clearing the floorboards for new feet to pass over. At the front desk he waited in anticipation—of what, he did not know, never having been in a hotel before. The door slammed shut again, and the man with the broom stood behind him.

"Go ahead, ring the bell," he said.

JT searched the counter and found a silver desk bell resting on top. His hand hovered over it for a moment, then he pressed down, his fingers jumping back quickly when it issued a shrill ding. He removed his hat and stepped back from the bell.

"Hold your horses, sugar," a voice came from the back. Through beaded curtains stepped a middle-aged woman, heavy boned and curvaceous. Her plumped thickness disguised a pretty face framed with burnished hair that could fool most in the muted lights of a saloon. When she caught sight of JT, her face brightened.

"Well, what have we here? A real live cowboy." Her elbows rested on the table, her chin cupped in both hands.

"Good mornin'—I mean—good afternoon ma'am."

"And a real live gentleman to boot. What's your name, sugar?"

"JT Swain, ma'am."

"Well, JT Swain, what is it I can do for you?" Her hand slid down the length of her neck to the top of her ample bosom.

"Yes, ma'am," he said, gripping his hat tighter. "I'd like to see about a room."

She sighed, lifting her elbows from the counter and picked up a pen laying on top. "A room, is it? How many nights?"

"Just one."

"Single or double occupancy?"

"Ma'am?"

"Are you sleeping alone or do you have company?"

"Oh for hell's sake, Cora. Leave the boy alone. You can see he's by himself." The man's words came from the back room.

"Shut your trap, Carl," she said, twisting her face into a frown. "I knows that." She turned back towards JT and smiled. "Just having me a little fun, that's all."

"Just be me in the room," he said.

"Single occupancy." She made another mark in the book. "Have yourself a horse?"

He nodded.

"At the livery stables?"

"Yes ma'am."

"That'll be $2.00 for the room and fifty cents for the stables. Anything else?"

"Yes ma'am. I'd like to pay for a hot bath."

"One bath," she said, writing it down. "That will be two bits." Her eyes traveled from his head to his toes. "I see you'll need an extra-large tub on account of your ... feet," she said.

JT looked down at his boots.

She laughed. "It's okay, sugar."

She handed him room key No. 5 and directed him up the stairs. Her husband Carl would be up momentarily with hot water for the bath.

"You be sure to holler if you need help."

"Yes ma'am," he said, unsettled as her eyes followed him up the stairs.

The heat of the bath drew ahhhhs from the deep recesses of his throat as he lowered himself into the tub. The water darkened his tanned forearms and washed from it the miles of earth stretched across his skin. Baptized in its warmth his mind drifted, the smoothness of the porcelain cool against his neck. He couldn't conceive when the next time he could give himself over to such luxury, and what the shape of things would look like going forward. Fate sometimes crouches down and whistles low, faint enough for a body to ignore it if they choose. It's tempting to turn away. JT often had the feeling that the only way to appreciate what's to come is by looking behind at all that's gone before and see how life's events threaded themselves together. If that was true, maybe they were already rolled out in front of him, waiting for him to sew a line through them. But it was hard to have that kind of faith when the path ahead looked spent. Looking behind, all he could remember were the vultures circling the cairn in the ravine where he buried the stray. He was relieved in that regard. Relieved he knew where she was, knew she wasn't in pain, and if he did it right, those buzzards would be hard pressed to drag their dinner from under those weighty rocks.

The water was cold when he woke and the full moon hung outside his window, its shimmer bright enough to make light of the shadows in the room, but dark enough to remind him he had paid good money for a bed. By mercy he was going to use it.

D etermined to get his money's worth, he tried to sleep in, but the sun had trained him well to rise when she did. Mid-morning after breakfast he set out to collect Ruby. Rounding the corner of the livery stables, he was surprised to find the old Mexican in the stall speaking Spanish into her ear. The saddle was positioned on her back and the Mexican tightened the cinch against her belly. Once secured he waited until she relaxed, then tightened it again. Ruby's head turned as JT stepped into the stall. The Mexican reached his hand along her mane and stroked her neck.

"Buenos días, señor," JT said.

"Buenos días." The old man bowed his head. Lifting the bridle from the hook, he felt for the bit and then brought it towards the horse. He slid the bridle over her face with his left hand behind her ears and pressed down on the poll until she lowered her head, then released. Holding the bridle by the cheek strap he gently nudged the bit against her muzzle until she opened her mouth and allowed the metal to slide between her teeth. All the while he murmured softly into her ears.

"Su caballo es muy linda."

"Hear that Ruby? You've got an admirer." JT grinned, stroking her muzzle.

"¿Señor?"

"Sí, es bonita, gracias. ¿Cuánto?"

The Mexican shooed the air. "Nada, nada." He smiled, revealing a row of three teeth.

JT walked into the stall and tapped Ruby's right foreleg, pulling it up to examine the shoe. He did the same to the back leg. The smithy did a first-rate job and he admired the craftsmanship.

"Por favor, tome esto por su tiempo."

The Mexican shook his head, but JT gently deposited two pesos in his hand, curling the man's fingers around the coins.

The old man nodded and bowed. "Gracias, señor, gracias."

JT gathered the reins and walked Ruby from the stall, the man trailing behind. As he saddled up, the hollered sounds of whooping reached his ears. It came from the far end of town.

"¿Qué pasa?" he said.

"El rodeo. Adiós señor. Vaya con dios."

The rodeo was a queer thing, a makeshift corral that sagged in places where previous riders had butted up or been thrown against the side. Wood splintered in sections of the pen while the muddied ground lay caked with manure and piss and strewn pieces of straw ticking. It looked worn and tired, and JT imagined it had seen its share of bronc and bull busting over the course of its lifetime. He sidled closer to the crowd, receiving looks from the vaqueros who sat atop the fence. They glanced at him with mild disinterest, then back at the ring.

Out of the chute came a kid who looked to be no more than 12 years old, riding a bull. The bull's horns were sawed down and tape covered the tips, no doubt to guard against gouging. The rider had his left hand high in the air, the other wrapped tightly around the rope. JT saw that the kid had the rope wound too tight for bronc riding. *Don't do that*, he said in his head. *When that bull starts to spin, he'll bring you down into the well and kill you outright.* And no sooner did he think it, than the animal started fading, leaning into the spin and gaining ground in tight circles. He looked at the crowd. They seemed not to notice—or not to care. JT motioned to the young boy at the gate to open it, then he and Ruby entered the ring.

A hush came over the crowd. Then boos and hissing. He brought Ruby close to the bull in the direction the animal was bucking, then yelled at the boy to loosen the rope. The kid acted like he didn't hear. JT yelled again, but the rider ignored him. He moved closer 'til they were side by side. The bull snorted, leaping high into the air and throwing down into a sunfish, trying to toss the rider off. To his credit the kid leaned back in the arc of the jackknife to regain his balance when the bull flipped back. The bull was an arm jerker for sure and he watched the kid bounce on the animal like a straw doll. Ruby was getting spooked and JT knew time was short. He closed in and grabbed the kid around the waist. The kid loosened his grip on the rope and JT pulled him free, the cord unraveling as the boy's hand opened to free it, minutes before the bull faded and rolled. When it came to its feet, the vaqueros opened the chute and coaxed the bull back into the holding pen. JT slowed Ruby and brought the half hanging kid to the ground. The kid struggled against him and pushed back from the horse, hitting the fence and toppling onto the mucked floor of the corral.

The crowd tittered and gave JT a healthy round of applause. He took off his hat and rounded the corral, tipping his head in mock appreciation, not wholly understanding what was so funny, but soaking it up all the same. On his way around he noticed the rider's hat on the ground and scooped it up by leaning way out of the saddle. This was greeted by more applause and yahooing. He carried it full circle to where the kid had fallen. There he found himself staring into the green eyes of a fire, accompanied by a stream of Spanish—none of which he could understand. The venom in the tone, however, was unmistakable.

"Who the hell are you?"

Standing before him in chinos and black baggy pants was a girl. JT took off his hat.

"¿Senorita?"

"Why did you do that?"

"What? Save your life?"

"Ha!" She spat on the ground. "I need no saving from you, jackass."

A high murmur came from the crowd, followed by catcalls and whooping.

"Your idiot horse spooked my bull," she said.

He could not take his eyes from the fire blazing before him.

"I am truly sorry, miss." He said this with genuine regret and handed her the hat.

"Yes," she said, snatching it out of his hand, "you truly are." She stomped off, turning from a distance to yell "imbécil" in his direction.

He watched her go, hair flying out behind her in waves of flame. A hand came to rest on his shoulder.

"You have had your first encounter with a wildcat, my friend," a man's voice said, pointing a finger in the girl's direction.

"You knew it was a girl?"

"Sí, claro. She's a regular here." He clapped JT's shoulders with both hands. "Take heart, amigo, you have been mauled by a wildcat and live to tell about it.

You are stronger than most." He smiled and turned to leave.

"Wait," JT said, not wanting to look away from the girl. "Who is she?

"Everyone knows. Dalia Jackson. From the Paraíso Ranch in Cruces."

5.

When I was ten, I rode with my father to the rim of his land. We stood the horses on the crest of the rise, above the rolling grasslands where the valley below was dotted with the white horns of grazing cattle, and in the far distance buzzards swam in circles over the rotting carcasses of misfortunate creatures expiring in the maddening heat. His arm swept the vista and he warned me to never forget this is where I come from. Never forget our past shapes us in ways not fully understood until well past the time it has shaped us and respect that we don't know the whole truth of how this happens, but know that it does. He explained that the nature of all things comes from the earth, and from it strength and purpose. Without it we are motes caught in the shaft of a beam, perpetually moving but going nowhere. He told me that people's lives lead them to crossroads that surprise them in many ways and that it is the journey that chooses them, not the other way around. We may think the opposite, but we would be wrong. "Those who do well are the ones who accept this truth." He asked if I understood, and I said I did.

After he spoke we sat the horses for a long time without words and watched the land stretch out before us. I felt an unbelievable surge of pride, knowing this great man was my father, my protector. His love was tangible then. I felt its weight, the space it occupied in my heart. When I think back on that day I am moved by how fleeting pride can be and how easily I succumbed to its power. It now comes as no surprise that he asked if I understood. He could not conceive, even then, of a woman's thirst for the land. I now know that the words he spoke were meant for a son's ears, not a daughter's.

All remained right in my world the remainder of that year, and the ones after that, until I reached the age of thirteen and my father remanded me to the house where I stamped my feet and raged and carried on like a prisoner jailed for a crime I did not commit. At these times he scolded my mother, insisting she failed in her duty to make his daughter understand her obligations in this life, a result of leaving me unchecked far too long. Words that drummed my ears and made my head light. I often wonder, when did this happen? When did what I was, became more important to him than who I was.

I begged my mother, "How can you let him make these choices for me? How can you allow him to tie me to this house, these clothes that bind my breath and demand I be something different, someone I am not?" My mother's eyes wearied with surrender. I threw myself at her feet, wailing for my abuela, insisting she was the only one who understood me. But my mother grabbed my arm and pulled me from the floor. "You are wrong," she said. "Your abuela had no understanding of the events she set in motion when choosing to fix her granddaughter's totem in the earth. It is she who cursed you, destining for a woman the desires of a man in a man's world. The sooner you make peace with the choices given you, the sooner you will find happiness."

"And you mother? Have you found happiness?"

No sooner had these words left my lips than my mother's hand came up to meet them, striking my face for the first time in my life, the slap as sharp as the anger behind it. I felt the slow burn steal across my skin, the momentary numbness take hold. Poised to strike me a second time, my mother's hand remained upraised, the fingers twitching, the whole of her trembling. Tears filled my eyes but I remained unflinching, my pain awake but the whole of me defiant. My mother's hand dropped. She turned and left the room. Something in the way she stooped signaled to me the sacrifices she endured in this marriage to my father and to this way of life. Still, I pushed it away, too puerile and self-involved to allow my mother this kindness.

T he voices downstairs carry upstairs, and I open my bedroom door the width of one eye to better hear the words between them. As usual, my father dominates the conversation. It is hard to make out my mother's voice in the midst of his maelstrom.

"You don't have to tell me this. Yes, she is good with stock. But she cannot be riding wild horses outside of this ranch like a common cowhand. I'll be damned if a daughter of mine will be seen tramping into a ring with vaqueros whooping and hollering at her."

My mother's voice is an inaudible whisper to my ear.

"But it's your job to know where she is and what she's doing. Dammit woman. How many times do I have to say this?"

My mother speaks, but still I cannot make out her words. There is a lull in the conversation and the house lays still. Too still. I know this place. The eye of the twister when everything is quiet and at its most dangerous. I hear my father's feet shift on the hardwood floors. When he speaks again, his voice is different. It has turned hard, and my mother's accompanied silence tells me she recognizes the change.

"I'm going to pretend I didn't hear you say that, Nelli," my father says, calling my mother by her Nahua birth name. There is another space of dead air and no movement from below.

"I do not want my daughter, nor will I ever again hear of her, in a rodeo anywhere, anytime, while she lives in this house, understood?" There is a pause in which I imagine my mother nodding. "Good. Because if you can't control her, I'll see to it she takes up residence at St. Augustine's for her schooling—and trust me, they'll wrestle the defiance from her."

His boots carry across the room, each step pronouncing its threat on the polished floor. I listen for my mother's footsteps to follow, but there are none. I picture my mother standing alone, staring into the fire, the lightness of her body lending the absence of weight to the room.

M y quinceañera is planned in two days' time. The guest list is long, some who are ranchers from neighboring towns. Some I know and some I do not, and amongst those I do not is a man who does business with my father. This man has asked about me after seeing my picture, a gesture which my father offered up while transacting business.

"Be on your best behavior."

"Yes, Papá."

"This man is coming a long ways to meet you."

"I thought he was *your* guest."

"He is my guest. Everyone who comes into this house is my guest. But he has a particular interest in meeting you."

"Why?"

"Dammit Dalia, don't play coy with me. You know why."

I do not look away. "I'm not ready."

"For heaven's sake, darlin'. He's not going to steal you away. He wants to court you, that's all."

"Does it matter what I want?"

My father shifts his gaze to the end of the table where my mother sits stoically stirring her soup, her head bowed.

"I'm your father. I know what's best for you."

"If you knew me, I might believe that."

His fist hits the table with such force that gravy spills from the serving bowl.

"Where does this disrespect come from?" His voice rises quickly, roughly, and I watch him strain to control his temper. Finally he pushes his chair back from the table and leaves the room, his dinner half-eaten. My mother quickly stands and moves to remove his plate.

That evening my mother adjusts the red sash on my white chiffon dress in front of the bedroom dressing mirror as I stand on a stool. The dress rests high on my waist and I stare, unblinking, at the reflection in the mirror. I notice for the first time, now that I am out of chinos and men's tailored shirts, that my body curves in places I did not appreciate before. How odd I feel on this pedestal peering at the image of a young woman I do not recognize. The corset is bound too tight, and I resent the exercise required to breathe. On my feet are the hard-black shoes that bind me further, their shiny patent leather begging to be dulled by use. I have stood this way for nearly an hour and now shift my feet to spell them from the strain.

"Dalia. Stay still."

"Mamá, how old were you when you married Papá?"

My mother continues to work on the sash, looking up briefly to meet my eyes.

"16."

"And Papá. How old was he?"

"Your father was 33 years when we wed."

I do the math in my head. "It did not bother you that he was so much older?"

Her mother pulls the sash's fabric tight across my waist. "What is there to bother about?" she says. "15 years is not so many to concern oneself with."

"17," I correct her.

My mother looks into the mirror, inspecting my appearance. "You were always good in arithmetic," she says.

"Did your parents not object to your marriage to a white man?"

I wait, but my mother remains silent, retying the sash's bow at my waist.

"Mamá?"

"Your abuela's first husband was white. He died fighting during the Mexican War on the side of the Nahua."

This is a lie. My abuela was raped by a white man. I know this because two years ago I overheard a discussion between my father and his mother, Grandmamá. This is how I know my mother is a half-breed.

"Your father is a great man and well respected among my people. He too fought with the Nahua alongside Zapata during the revolution against Diaz. Because of this my father consented to his request for my hand in marriage."

Another lie. It is true my father fought during the revolution. I also know that he saved my mother's youngest brother from drowning. It was for this reason that my Nahua grandfather gifted my mother's hand in marriage to a white man. This too I overheard from Grandmama.

"And you have not once looked back?"

My mother pauses and looks to the window. We have never spoken of these things and for a moment I think I have reached a place inside her, softened a hardness there. My mother turns to me, a pressed smile on her face.

"What is there to look back to? It is now dust."

My mother fingers the puffed sleeves, pulling them down over the curve of my shoulders so my skin peeks out. Brown against the white dress. "There. Is that not beautiful?" There is levity in her voice, but her lips have released their smile. I look in the mirror and do not recognize the young woman with bared shoulders in front of me. I look at the reflection of the woman behind me and see myself, fifteen years from now.

6.

Ruby dipped her head and tightened the slack in the reins as they stood solemn on the crest of the rise above the Mesilla Valley, the breadth of the hacienda rolled out below them. JT whistled under his breath and wiped the sweat from his brow with his sleeve. It was now unclear if this made as much sense to him as it had earlier that morning when he set out to find the Paraíso Ranch.

After their stomp in the rodeo pen, JT noticed a limp in Ruby's gait, the way she favored her left foreleg and kept weight off the right. The sole of her foot was stone bruised. Not badly, but she'd need a good ten days to two weeks before he could make her bear his weight across the plains in six to eight hour stretches. She needed rest, and the idea of finding work and making money while they waited made sense. Besides, he was hungry to see this ranch that the vaqueros kept crowing about. And it crossed his mind that it would be a decent thing to apologize one more time to Dalia Jackson. These things crowded his thoughts as he traveled the five miles from the town of Mesilla to Las Cruces. Yet as he stood above the valley looking down on the ranch, his misgivings gave way.

Las Cruces had a familiar feel to it, like he had been here before, or slept there in a memory once. Hell, maybe another lifetime. He knew his brother would laugh if he heard him say this. It brought a memory to mind a couple weeks after Ma died when he and Harlan were laying in their beds. They got to talking about dying while a soft drizzle winded outside. JT was only ten at the time so Harlan must have been thirteen. He asked Harlan if he believed in heaven and hell and what he thought of all that reincarnation stuff then listened to him say it all amounted to the same.

"How do you mean?" JT said.

"You're dead, you're dead. And anyways, if you come back you don't get to remember your other life, so it's like it don't exist anyways."

JT thought on that awhile. "Are you sure?"

"It's what I believe."

"I'd just like to know, that's all."

"Hell, we'd all like to know. My saying it ain't gonna make it so. It don't work that way."

They lay silent for a spell, and then JT spoke again. "Where do you think we go when we die?"

"Who knows? Don't matter none 'cause it's gonna happen whether we worry about it or not. Shoot, we might be going to a big ol' horse ranch up in the sky. Now go to sleep."

"In the sky?" JT grinned. "What kind of ranch would that be?"

"Someplace we don't have to worry about dying I guess. Hell, I don't know."

A fiery crack of lightning came close to the window and made JT jump. Harlan laughed.

"Go to sleep."

Harlan turned in the bed, his back to his brother. JT lay quiet wondering about the possibilities. After a few minutes, his brother's voice reached out to him in the dark.

"What?"

"What?"

"What is it?"

"Nothing."

"Better go ahead and say it."

"It's nothing."

"I won't sleep 'til you say it, so let's get it done."

JT was reluctant to voice his thoughts out loud about the newly dead.

"Where do you think Ma's gone to?" he whispered.

"Same place we're going, I hope. Just not so soon."

"What about Pa? Where will he go when he dies?"

Nothing came from Harlan's side of the bed. JT waited.

"I can't pitch judgment over Pa. I can only hope it's not the same place I'm going."

"Do you think Granddad will be with Ma when he goes?"

"For sure. If there's a heaven, I know they will. They'll be waiting on us when it's our turn. I'll put *that* in writing. Now get some sleep."

All this ran through JT's head as he sat overlooking the Paraíso Ranch and thinking what kind of man makes the kind of money to own a ranch like this and gets to live his heaven right here and now. And he couldn't help wondering if he himself was ever going to see that kind of heaven in his future. His future on earth, that is.

H e walked Ruby carefully along the dusted trail leading down to the ranch and made his way towards the main corral. A man stood in the center, his back to JT, working a string of horses. JT watched him work, the way he controlled the herd using the whip he held, barely cracking it. Its presence alone commanded the horses' attention. JT noticed a ring of keys hung from a belt loop around his waist. He swung down out of the saddle.

"Howdy."

The man turned his head to look at him, then turned back towards the horses.

"Hola amigo. ¿Como estas?"

JT waited, then tried once more.

"Eres el jefe?"

"I speak English, asshole." The man said this from the center of the pen, his attention still on the horses. JT rested his arms on the top of the corral's post.

"Who does a cowboy need to speak to about hiring on?"

The man turned to look at him. "Cowboy?" A broad smile broke across his face and he laughed, a loud braying sound that exploded from his chest.

"Domingo. Ven aquí. Come look at the cowboy."

Another Mexican, rake in hand, emerged from the stables. He came close to the edge of the corral and looked JT up and down, wiping his mouth with the back of a sweat stained sleeve. Then he spoke to the man in the ring, never taking his eyes off JT.

"Donde? Where is the cowboy? I see no cowboy."

The man in the corral leaned his head back and laughed, then turned back towards the horses.

"Go home, cabrón," Domingo said. "We do not hire niños."

He made to leave but JT walked Ruby in front of him, blocking his path.

"Is that so, amigo? Let me show you a thing or two this child can do."

JT dropped the reins in the Mexican's hands, then turned and walked towards the corral.

He was two feet from the gate when Domingo's hand grabbed him by the shoulder and yanked him around. The Mexican's fist swung hard and caught the side of JT's jaw. Pain exploded in his head as he doubled down in the dirt.

"I'm not your stable boy, amigo," Domingo said, throwing the reins in JT's face and kicking his leg out from under him as he tried to get up. Ruby backed away and JT slid to the ground. Domingo's boot rose above his face. As it came down JT grabbed hold of the foot, balancing his strength against the man's weight, and twisted. Domingo hit the ground, yelling as he fell. When he raised his head, JT saw blood on his lips. Domingo used the same dirty sleeve to wipe his mouth, taking stock of the blood as he did. A dark fury settled in his eyes. "I will kill you."

JT stepped back as Domingo came at him, swinging his left fist, then his right. The boy raised his left arm and blocked the Mexican's punch, then used his right hand to plant a fist on the side of the man's head. Domingo roared as he staggered back.

"Look—" JT said. But Domingo leapt forward and pummeled him with both fists, then kicked JT backwards, slamming him into the side of the corral. The sound of wood splintering upset the ponies and they ran from the dust as JT fell backwards into the pen. It knocked the wind from him and he struggled to breathe. Out of the dust Domingo came bearing down, a wildness in his eyes JT hadn't seen since Pa died. When the man reached down to grab him, JT lifted his legs to Domingo's chest, and flipped him over, head first, onto the dirt. Domingo landed on his back, his lungs flattened. JT stood and leaned his hands on his knees, catching his breath and feeling a wrench in his right shoulder. Domingo lay dazed sucking air. JT walked toward him, watching him wheeze, then stuck out his hand. The Mexican grabbed hold, but as JT pulled him up, Domingo sucker punched him with the other. JT doubled forward and Domingo buried a fist below his left eye. The impact pitched JT backwards against the water trough, spilling the whole of it over the corral floor. Immediately JT felt the shiner swell up, and in what was left of his sight he could see Domingo come at him again. He scrabbled backwards, trying to make room, and as the Mexican stepped closer, JT's feet pushed the empty trough in front of him. It smacked into Domingo's legs hard and the man stumbled, wildly trying to regain his balance, then fell into the thick mud from the trough spill. He landed face first in the muck, then came up swearing, everything on him plastered shit brown. JT grinned when the words flying out of Domingo's mouth were mud, but his smile faded fast when he realized the man wasn't done with him.

A crowd gathered. Several of the cowhands and vaqueros came from their roosts, wondering what all the commotion was about, then settled in to enjoy the show. When Domingo fell into the mud, hoots of laughter broke out together with clapping. This only served to infuriate the Mexican. He came at JT in a rage, swinging wide, flecks of mud springing off his fists onto the boy's face and clothes. JT ducked, and with a right punch knocked Domingo back into the mud where he landed face up. Then JT came at him, determined to end this. But suddenly he was flying as his feet slipped out from underneath him. He too landed on his back in the mud. There was more laughter and words in Spanish that JT could not make out. As he tried to get up, he was slammed back down feeling Domingo's weight squarely on top of him. They rolled side-to-side, their hands trying to grab hold of each other, slipping from their grips like well-oiled pigs. At one point their eyes and mouth were so caked with the stuff, JT thought he had gone blind and buried until he spat out a huge chunk and continued on. It wasn't clear, not even to the vaqueros, who was who. So covered in brown soaked grime, they could almost be twins.

Domingo got hold of JT's shirt collar and pulled him close enough so that he could smell the tequila on the Mexican's breath, reminding JT that he was going to die, when a jerk of water flew out of nowhere and struck them square in their chests. It hit them with such force that they both flew backwards against the side of the corral. The burst of its power blinded them, and it kept on coming. A man stood wielding an industrial sized water hose, the kind they use in case of fire, and he had it trained on one of them, and then the other, back and forth. They stood there, being flailed by the water, yelling at him to stop. JT felt like his skin was about to blister and peel back. Finally the water turned off, and they both slid down against the fence, breathing heavy, the bulk of the mud cleared from their eyes and thrashed from their clothes. JT turned his head to look at Domingo, dragged out and beat, but damn if the man didn't make moves to come towards him. This time he looked like he was moving in slow motion. The wildness was gone from his eyes, but JT knew he meant to make right on his threat. The Mexican with the belt loop of keys stepped forward and held his hand stretched out towards Domingo.

"Basta."

Domingo paused, then spat in JT's direction. He moved back against the boards and slowly slid back down to the muddied ground. A great burst of applause went up from the crowd. JT weakly joined them.

The foreman looked the boy over with a half-smile. "A cowboy, huh? We shall see." He walked away, shaking his head. JT called after him.

"Does that mean I'm hired?"

The man stopped and turned. "Maybe yes, maybe no. You can see Señor Jackson up at the house. He owns the ranch. He decides who is hired and who is not."

JT picked himself up, feeling the water squish between his toes in the seat of his boots. He started to walk towards the house, but the foreman stopped him.

"If you show up like this," his hand dropped away across the front of him, "maybe no. A shower first. Then go see him. That is, unless you are un tonto, a *fool*."

The men yahooed behind him.

"Where do I …"

"At the bunk house. Over there." The man pointed to a short-roofed dwelling a few yards away. "Jesús, show the cowboy the way."

"Gracias." JT said. He picked his hat up and squared it on his head, then tried to straighten his back as he followed Jesús to the bunkhouse. A peep of chickens crowded his path and he made his way through, kicking his feet to scatter them. Behind him he heard the men talking to the foreman in Spanish about some kind of fiesta taking place. But he could not make out the words, his ears still tamped with mud.

7.

i am the only child of an only daughter, born to a ninth daughter. Evil nine, so unlucky a number, abuela forbids me to voice it while learning to count. Nine is the reason she suffers great loss in this life. Loss that follows her to the next if she is not careful. She tells me this while hanging the dead towhees and rock wrens by their feet in the trees surrounding the hacienda, coaxing me to do the same. Evening's cool loosens the smell of juniper in the air.

"Why song birds, abuelita?"

"Their music tempers Coatlicue."

"Who is she?"

Abuelita grabs my arm sharply and draws me to her. "Shush child ... do not say such things out loud." We crouch in the shade of the trees. She releases her hand against my mouth. "Creator and destroyer, the one skirted with snakes who crushes the heads of serpents."

Cursed nine, the number of underworlds beneath the earth, the dwelling of the dead. Snakebitten nine, the reason abuelita fears eternity as a phantom, scouring the earth. A fear she believes will translate to my own destiny if I am not careful. And because I feel her presence, the closeness of her spirit now, in the living, I pray with great seriousness that she has not become the lost ghost she had feared.

They come from all quadrants of the neighboring counties, some as far north as Lincoln, others as far west as Hildalgo. They come on horseback, in cars, but most come in trucks boiling in the tyrannical heat, clouds of smoked dust coating the sides of their vehicles. Behind the laced curtains of my bedroom I watch them procession the creased folds of road leading to the ranch, a large serpent threading its belly against the earth. They pass under the lettered Paraíso sign and drive forward between the rows of pecan trees, through the unlatched gate leading to the hacienda. Eduardo stands near a flat of roped off field and directs them to park, his chacabana and linen pants brushed tan from dirt kicked up by grinding tires. A yahoo leans out the window and waves his hat before disappearing inside the truck's cab. Eduardo's eyes follow the man's wave to my window, and I step back into my room.

Here is where my childhood lived, where my imagination dreamed the possibilities of life outside these walls, where my adoration for Papá flourished and withered. It was my fortress, then my prison—he my protector, then my warden. There is pain in that loss, a place here and inside that dwells on the reasons for change, the adapting to it. It's as if, for the parent, there is no accounting for the changeling before them who grew up as they requested, but who failed them by not remaining the same. Part of me wishes I could recapture the child who saw only nobleness in her father, while the other knows I can never go back.

My reflection in the full-length mirror makes me uneasy, in awe of the woman I see. I recognize my mother, the rouged face and faint red on the lips. ("Not too much," Grandmama says, "or she will look like a *puta*.") I see Grandmama, the hair brushed and pulled back from the face to strengthen the arch of my cheekbones. Who am I? Even the small scar above my left eyebrow where the horse threw me is hidden by makeup.

A barrette holds my hair in place, and it spills over bare skin where the sleeves of the chiffon dress dip slightly off the shoulders. I turn around and look back in the mirror to see the scooped back, then purse my lips. A married woman, a wife. The idea is ridiculous, yet I am the only one who sees it. Hours before at the church my sleeves were drawn up and covered by a white laced shawl, a gift from my mother. The shawl she wore on her quinceañera. Abuelita spoke often of this day, my transition from child to adult, from girl to woman, forewarning me it is a time I am expected to reflect upon my childhood blessings and sensibly face future challenges that await me. My choices are slim: live the ministry of religion or marry into the world of domestic servitude. As I see it, both are prison sentences.

I am consulted very little in preparation for the party, because I am told I lack the enthusiasm to honor the quinceañera tradition. This is true. My Grandmamá sought to downplay the cultural proprieties, not wanting to draw attention to my Nahua roots. And although my mother won out in this regard, a triumph of extraordinary proportions, I refused to choose a *corte de honor* nor would I agree to be fitted with a crown. I will not enlist a circus. In return for these concessions I allow them to drape the customary sash pinned with the 15 red roses over me, but only for the church ceremony. Afterwards I hand it to the niñas in the church playground who parade the perimeter of the park enacting their own coming-of-age fiestas, too young to appreciate its noose-like qualities.

Before leaving the church I kneel before the image of Our Lady of Guadalupe, bow my head and impassion a silent plea for help. *Por favor, Virgin Mary, help me to escape the direction of my life. Grant me salvation by freedom. This I ask, through Christ our Lord, Amen.* I lay the bouquet of white peonies at her feet, an offering too small for such a large request.

M y father argued that I should greet the guests, but Grandmama prevailed in this matter. "She should make an entrance," his mother said, "after guests have arrived, befitting a young lady her stature." These are words designed to bolster my confidence and school me in the art of the reveal. But resentment grows hot under my skin at the thought of being paraded in front of suitors like a prized heifer. Men whose hunger smolders in their eyes and who exercise their fingers as though warming to break a horse, not play a delicate instrument. Bidders throwing their hats in the ring to compete for the prize, a piece of the rancher's land and the whole of his daughter. "Remember not to smile too wide," Grandmama instructed, "leave something to the imagination."

The knock on the door is soft, a gentle tap. Papá is dressed in a black suit and bolo, hair smoothed back, large hands gripping the brim of his hat. He swallows and stares at me. A slow smile spreads across his face.

"I'm looking for my daughter. Have you seen her?"

"Oh, Papá." As miserable as I am playing this part, I savor the moment. It has been a long time since my father smiled completely in my direction. Here we are, on opposite sides of a threshold, each seeing the other as something they are not. The tamed rebellious daughter, the pedigreed doting father. Perhaps if we don't move, we will stay this way forever. I wish this with all my heart, to remain in my father's favor. Yet how can I be what I am not?

"Que bonita." His voice is quiet, almost a whisper. "Shall we?" He holds out his arm. I slip mine through his and we stand close, feeling the weight of our bodies touch. "Wait. I almost forgot." He pulls a cream-colored box from his pocket and hands it to me. Inside is a hairpin made from abalone, the iridescent mother-of-pearl shell set in an oval shape. A slender stick of wood is slipped through the row of holes in the shell's outer edge.

"Your abuela's. A gift from her father on her 15th birthday. Your mother wants you to have it."

I remember this hairpin. I saw it many times in my mother's jewelry box, but never in my mother's hair. It is one of the last reminders she has of her mother. My fingertips glide over the shell, colors that shift as the light strikes. Natural in its simplicity, like abuelita. There is sadness wrapped up in this gift. I wish it were not given to me on this, of all days. For I know abuelita would spit the ground if she knew the plans put in place. But how can I refuse? I hand the hairpin to Papá, reach behind my head and remove the barrette, then face the mirror.

"I'm all thumbs at this kind of thing, darlin'." He holds the shell in place and pushes the wood through the holes. I feel the tension take up in my hair. When I raise my head our mirrored image faces us. Can he see it? I do. The patriarch and the rebel, the guardian and the guarded. It is one of the last clear memories I will take with me. In the mirror I see my childhood still warm behind me, the muñeca lying on my quilted bed, presented by my padrinos, my godparents, as a gift at the church, el ultimo juguete. The last doll of my adolescence. I long to fracture the mirror's glass, to erase the past and future—just be me, in the present. But broken mirrors are as dangerous as the number nine. I will miss this room, these walls, the cindered smell of adobe brick laid at my feet during the night, the sweet flavor of Papá's pipe. But mostly I worry whether Lucas will visit my dreams if I am not here when I dream them.

We descend the stairs together and movement in the house quiets. At the bottom of the stairs, my father clears his throat.

"Ladies and Gentlemen. May I present my daughter, Dalia Jackson." My face flushes as a small titter of clapping takes place and Papá leads me to the parlor, nodding at guests as we pass.

There are a few boys I recognize from school, their mouths agape at the costume I wear. But mostly I see men much older whom I do not recognize. They are too seasoned to stare and have learned to veil their leering. The musicians pick up their instruments and begin to play while my father guides me across the hardwood floor. We dance a waltz, his arms lifting me nearly from the floor.

"Papá?"

"Yes?"

"Why can't it stay like this forever?"

"What's that?"

"You, me, Mamá. Living at Paraíso. Together."

He nods at fellow dancers as we pass, then dips his head closer to my ear.

"Let's not start, Dalia."

"But Papá ..."

His arms tighten and he steers me towards a corner of the room. Before I can protest, I am handed to Captain Charles Percy.

"Take good care of her Captain."

"You can be certain."

I stare after my father, the broadness of his shoulders, the smiles he offers to acquaintances who clamor for his attention. I watch as his form gets smaller the farther he moves away. Then I feel a slight pressure at my back, the cold feel of his fingers through the fabric of my dress as the Captain maneuvers me around the dance floor. His hand slips above the rim of my dress, cold fingers against my skin. I'm not repulsed by the touch, but by the idea that it conveys. The leading, commanding me, as if I am a young colt who needs to be taken by the halter and led forward. Establishing command from the outset so there is no question who is in control—a tactic I recognize from watching my father conduct business.

"A keen man, your father."

I place my hand in his creased palm, and we move gently to the music, his eyes never from my face. Not an unhandsome man, but his posture speaks of military and formality and age. I see a lifetime of pulling on and off boots.

"And you, Captain Percy?"

"Charles, please."

"Do you think yourself keen?" It is a rude remark and I regret it the moment the words leave my mouth. However, the hint of an amused smile crosses the Captain's face, quite the opposite effect I intended.

"I aspire to your father's prodigiousness, if that is what you mean."

A movement in the dance draws our bodies close and I smell the aftershave of cologne, the strong vinegar of its sting, the stiffness of his five o'clock shadow on my cheek and yes, this time I do recoil, ever slight. As I twirl I see my mother in the corner of the room, gazing out the window. She is beautiful in the custom gown my father purchased for her, stiff and unyielding, a stranger in her own clothing. How it must have been for her, given to a man she hardly knew, a white man unlike any she had known. I will miss the way her washed hair smells in the morning, and the gentleness with which she brushes my hair.

"I'm sorry, what?"

"You look exquisite tonight."

"Thank you."

"Your father tells me you turn 15 in one week."

"I do."

"Tell me. What is it that you most desire for your birthday?"

Dare I tell him the truth? That the one thing, the only thing I wish for is my freedom. The freedom to not dance with middle-aged men who reek of cologne and lust, of their egos and ambitions.

"I haven't given it much thought."

"Well then. It will just have to be a surprise, won't it?"

My mother is no longer in the corner of the room and my eyes search for her. There, whispering with Rosalía, our kitchen help. I see them look to the door where my father stands talking, then watch as he disappears onto the veranda. The music ends and we bow, then the orchestra begins again.

"Excuse me Captain—"

"Charles."

"Excuse me, Charles. Thank you for the dance."

Before he can reply, I am gone through the crowded dance floor. From a window I see who my father is talking to and am shocked. How dare he? I hurry to the door to hear the last remnants of their conversation.

"I'd like to help you son, really I would. I just don't need another hand."

The screen door slams behind me as I step out onto the veranda.

"Dalia—" my father says.

"Why is he here, Papá?"

"Excuse me?"

I look the imbécil straight in the eye. "You do not belong here."

"What in Sam's name is going on here? "Where are your manners young lady?

"It's fine, sir. Your daughter and I have met."

"Send him away," I say.

My father's eyes narrow as he looks at both of us, one at a time.

"Is that so? Where did you two meet?"

Nobody speaks.

"Well I ain't getting any younger."

"In Cruces, sir. At the rodeo."

"At the rodeo," my father repeats.

"I thought she was in trouble—"

"I was not in trouble."

"I reckon I know that now." The boy's hands fiddled with his hat. "I thought that bull was going to take you down into a spin."

"Bull?" Papá's eyes widen.

"Imbécil."

"Dalia!"

"I'm sorry Papá, but this tonto—"

"You will keep a civil tongue in your mouth, young lady."

"This stranger had no business—"

"—saving your neck?"

"I need no saving."

My father sighs and shakes his head. "No, I don't imagine you think you do." He rubs his chin and looks from the imbecile to me, then back.

"Go tell the foreman to find you a bunk. We start before sun breaks."

"But Papá!" I stamp my patent leather shoes against the boards of the veranda.

"Hush, darlin'," my father says, escorting me back into the house. "Just think of it like having a guardian angel."

ime weighs heavy and I am exhausted. The evening is spent dancing with Captain Percy, except when I avoid being available. If he notices, he doesn't let on, proffering a smile and chivalrous bow when another suitor beats him to the quick. I dance with men who smell of tobacco and alcohol and listen to tiresome talk of livestock and drought while graciously turning down dinner proposals and picnics. Men whose hands reach below the curve of my waist, or above the small of my back, craving the touch of skin. Finally I escape.

Outside I breathe the quiet of the New Mexico sky. The moon hangs low on the shelf of the mountain, Tecciztecatl's efforts at atonement. A vagrant breeze crosses my cheek and with it I feel abuelita's kiss, and then it is gone. The brush of her lips carried on the wind both cheers and saddens me. I walk to the barn and listen to the horses talk as I offer up the cubes of sugar stolen from the kitchen. I slip my hands over their muzzles. They smell coarse and bricked from earth's clay. The gringo's roan neighs loudly and stretches her head from the stall. She is a fine horse, the muscled girth, the beauty of her lines. I move to her stall and offer the sugar, my hand stroking the strength of her neck.

"It's not your fault you belong to an imbécil."

"Don't I know it." A voice comes from the back of the stall.

My hand hesitates in mid-air, accompanied by a momentary flare of anger. But I am too tired and play along.

"Well then. Why don't you just run away?"

"Every time I buck him, he just comes back, like a bad penny.

I smile.

"He's the only family I got."

"Sometimes family ... sometimes you are better off on your own."

He walks out from the back of the stall, and continues to brush the horse, running it over her left flank.

"I don't know if that's rightly true," he says, "but it's probably not best to take advice from a horse."

"An imbécil's horse."

"Yeah, about that. I can't say as I wouldn't do it all again. Not with your hand in a suicide wrap like that."

"What?"

"Suicide wrap. When that bull faded into a spin, he would have taken you down. Trampled you."

There is truth in his eyes, but I am stubborn.

"It was none of your business."

"You're right miss, it was none of my business and I do apologize." He touches the brim of his hat. Music from the house trickles down to the barn. "Quite a shindig you got going on."

"Yes, my father's party."

He puts away the brush and halters the horse, then leads her out of the stall to a wheelbarrow of hay outside the barn door. I follow and we watch as the horse blows air from her nostrils and dips her head to eat.

"Why are you here?" I ask.

"Just passing through. Headed to California."

"California." I've heard of this place and its oceans of water.

"Ever been?"

"No."

"Me neither."

"How do you know you'll like it?"

"I don't."

I stare at this vaquero, this boy, who rides horses and thinks he rescues women. What would it be like, to have that kind of freedom? To decide your journey—not have it charted for you. To go someplace you've never been, not knowing if you'll ever return. Alone.

"But I reckon if I had a piece of land like this, California would be the furthest thing from my mind."

"Is that why you're here?"

"What—"

"To win a piece of the rancher's land?"

He looks at me, blank-eyed.

"I swear, I don't know what you're talkin' about."

Again, in his eyes I see truth.

"What would you know?" I say, less sharply than before. "You who have the freedom to go where you choose, do what you want, be who you want."

A burst of laughter from the party interrupts and we glance in the direction of the house. The stars rocket out beyond the night sky, the twinkling of The Great Hunter clean and clear. Moonlight leans into the space between our shadows.

"What's that?" he asks.

"What?"

"In your hair."

My hands reach behind and touch the hairpin. "A gift from my mother's mother. It's made of abalone shell. Would you like to touch it?"

I remove the pin and hand it to him. My hair falls and I push it from my face as he runs his thumb over the smooth shell. When he looks up, he stares at me strangely, as though I have just appeared.

"It's beautiful," he says, his voice different. Another shout of laughter drifts down from the hacienda and we turn toward the house.

"I suppose they'll want you back at the party."

And suddenly the thought of returning to the party, returning to the house, returning to the life laid out for me, a life I am condemned to, a thought seizes me so powerful I have to choke it back.

"Who cares what they want? This is the problem with men. Everything in life they want to control and think they can own. People, the land, the air."

"Now hang on. I didn't mean—"

"It is not enough to control your own lives, you must control everyone else."

I fumble with the gate, trying to open it.

"Dalia, wait." It is the first time he has said my name. I feel his presence behind me, his breath against my hair. "There's truth in that," he says, his voice soft. He pauses, then let's go of his words. "But being on your own isn't everything you think. Trust me."

I sense weariness in his voice and something else. Something deeper. He reaches in front of me and for a moment I think he means to narrow the gap between us. Then his hands carefully release the latch. The gate swings open.

"I should go," I say.

"Wait." He holds out his hand. "JT. JT Swain. Pleased to meet you."

I hesitate, then slip my fingers inside the palm of his hand.

"Good night JT Swain. Buenos noches."

Late that night Lucas comes to me in my dreams. He takes my hand and leads me to the river that flows through the veins of Las Cruces to the Rio Grande. I walk into the river where my abuela stands, waist deep in water. Lucas cannot swim, so he remains on the shore. White vapors float from the surface as she dips my head in stilled waters, the steam from our bodies rising in the stinging cold. Abuelita sings to the sky in Nahautl, words I recognize but do not understand. When we finish, Lucas holds out his hand from the shore. I turn to kiss abuelita but discover she is a water moccasin. The beauty of her body curls around the water's liquid, fluid and pure, as she disappears downriver. Then I grab hold of Lucas' hand and he lifts me from the water.

8.

araíso Ranch spanned 32,000 acres of Dona Ana County West Mesa in a northwest direction, its feet reaching into Picacho Peak at elevations of 5000 feet, carpeted in dry scrublands. Beyond its boundaries lay the Robledo Mountains lining the Rio Grande, juniper strewn across the volcanic cliffs and expansive desert grassland swales, its lowlands covered in creosote. The southern portions of the ranch were better irrigated with grassed vegetation on the plains where cattle shaded up under stands of black willow and cottonwood when the sun turned up its heat. Drought had brought the valley to its knees, and the basins that ran water waist deep two years before were dry as a dead hog in August. As he traveled north he saw tracks of fox, deer, and possibly black bear, though he doubted bear were running this far south. Clusters of late-blooming cholla dotted the otherwise neutral landscape scarlet. He stopped and watered the horse at a steel stock tank and rode on.

The spread was fenced in by barbed wire spaced five strands apart and anchored in the corners with H braced wood posts. A simple travois trailed behind the horse, constructed of two poles shafts and between them a stretched tarp that carried his tools—a hammer, shovel, and small saw, a pair of bolt-cutters and a fence jack, a coil of stay wire, extra staples, and a couple of newly sawed posts in the event one needed to be replaced. Each day he rode a narrow dirt trail cut by fence riders before him, searching for loose wires, gaps or holes, fallen posts, missing or dislodged staples, generally anything that compromised the security of the ranch. At night he bedded down under the stars, trying not to think about his life before—the pain of living with his father, the pain of living without Harlan—instead focusing on the future. He thought about the night he arrived at the ranch, losing his breath when she entered the barn, his pulse pounding in his ears. The way she loved horses.

It took him two days to canvass half the perimeter of the acreage and during that time he had spliced together more broken barbed wire than he cared to remember. Each repair required measuring out a piece of wire 4 feet longer than the existing gap in the broken wire, then attaching it to the left side of that strand making sure it overlapped by two or more barbs. He twisted it tight, then inserted the right side of the broken wire into a fence jack and clamped it. He did the same with the left side of the broken strand and clamped the jack wires tight again. The new wire was then wound around the existing right strand, again overlapping two or more barbs and tightened. He tied up the fence tag ends by winding them around the spliced wire. Any staples found missing in the adjacent posts also needed to be replaced. Fence-riding. It was a shit job. He knew it. Dalia's father knew it. And no doubt the drovers on the cattle drive were having themselves a good laugh about it.

He rode a small paint named Chica who had a bad habit of crossing her jaw, pulling up short and balking when least expected. The vaqueros had tried to break her of the jaw crossing by using a grakle, but JT replaced it with a noseband and worked to stop the horse's strong shoulders from setting by gentle give and take contact to encourage her to relax. It was a work in progress. The pulling up short and balking was a bigger nuisance. It frustrated JT, not knowing the horse beneath him. Granddad always said that getting in good with one horse—one companion who moved in rhythm with the rider as though they were of one mind—was worth their weight in gold. There's beauty in the way they communicate and how each understands that the slightest deviation from the routine signals a warning to be heeded. JT had been around horses long enough to recognize wisdom behind every dance, every twitch. The slightest indication something in Chica's world was amiss made her stop and announce it. He came to appreciate the acute sense she possessed of her surroundings when after a stalled moment of trying to move her forward, a diamondback slid out of the brush in front of them. After that he began to trust her intuition and allowed her some freedom in that regard, but never wholly since Granddad had always cautioned it served no purpose allowing a horse to think it could make decisions. Suggestions, yes. Decisions, no.

He crossed a wash where he noticed cattle circling a mud hole thick with flies and stinking of bogged dirt. Moving closer he saw a calf had ventured too close to the watery edge and was now sunk belly deep in mud. From the condition of the caked clay, it had been stranded a day or two. JT dismounted, untied the rope from his saddle, and secured one end to the horn and paid out the rest in the direction of the calf. He parted the cattle under marked consternation from the mother who bellered and reluctantly backed up. JT reached the yearling and buried down into the mud around the calf's front legs and up the other side to form a circle around the calf's belly, then tied a knot at the top of the neck and pulled it taut. He tugged on the rope to encourage the animal, then moved with it as Chica backed up. Calves this young were often too weak to survive a rescue, but this one had some feistiness left in him and bawled, struggling against the dragline. The mud gave off lewd sucking sounds as the legs came free. When it was a couple yards from the sinkhole he slacked the rope and the calf lay on its side panting while its mother moved closer, her tongue lapping at the animal's nose, clearing its mud caked nostrils. JT removed the rope and wound it, wiping the excess clay free as it coiled. By the time he finished, the calf was standing on shaky legs and suckling at its mother's teat. He mounted the horse and rode on.

He heard damage to the fence was worse on the northwest divide, beaten down by a dust storm late spring that drove a 40 ft. wall of debris across the Mesilla Valley, responsible for the death of two ranch hands and a number of livestock. It blacked out the entire sky. The vaqueros described it as *cortina de negro*, a curtain of black, so frightening that the evangelists preached Armageddon was at hand from pulpits strewn with dust.

The post anchoring the fence in the northwest pasture had snapped in two and hung by a splintered thread, the barbwire stretched out and the staples scattered. The bottom of the post stood joined to the block of cement fixing it in the ground. JT used the shovel to dig at the sides of the broken post, loosening the cement from its hold on the earth, then lifted it with cement intact and laid it on the ground. When he looked up, a cloud of dust in the distance chased a rider approaching from the west. JT retrieved a newly sawed post from the litter and laid it next to the splintered post on the ground, then retrieved the bolt cutters from his saddlebag. As he prepared to cut the tangled barbwire, the rider reined up on the other side of the fence.

"Who you working for, son?"

"William Jackson."

The man nodded. He sat the horse and looked out over the land.

"Bill's got a nice lay."

"Yessir."

JT severed the wire from the ends of the corner brace then measured it against the new post he would put in its place.

"Where's Jackson's hands?"

"Cattle drive."

"How come you ain't with 'em?"

"Drew the short stick."

The man threw back his head and laughed, lifting his hat and running his sleeve over his brow. His hair was peppered and thick and the way he sat the horse with assurance, his touch with the reins, reminded JT of Granddad.

"That about answers my next question."

"Sir?"

"How you makin' out with Jackson's men?"

JT tamped down the earth with the shovel.

"How about that pistol fired Mexican they have mucking out the stall. Sabado I think they call him. How's 'ol Sabado doing?"

JT smiled beneath the brim of his hat while he laid down the shovel on the ground, understanding he was being vetted. "You might be meaning Domingo."

The man studied JT for a moment then broke into a grin. "Damn, I believe you're right. Saturday, Sunday—whatever—I get them mixed up. How you two getting along?"

JT picked up the new pole and carried it to the closest line post where he measured it against the height of the existing column. With his pocketknife he marked a nick in the wood for how deep the post needed to set up in the hole. "All right."

"Mexican's got a temper," the man said, eyeing the yellowed bruises near JT's eye.

"A misunderstanding," JT said.

"Uh-huh." The man turned his head and spat. "Goin' to misunderstand himself right out of a job." He watched JT drag the pole back to the dug-out hole.

"You done this kind of work before?"

"Some."

"How you gonna set that post?"

JT shook his head.

"Ground be hard pressed to hold a fence post. Better off getting gravel from Box Canyon," the man said. "The old quarry mine, about 5 miles yonder. He pointed north. "Hell, wood is more likely to rot if set up in concrete." He put his thumb and forefinger to his hat, then touched the reins to back up the horse a few paces. "Good luck."

He turned the horse east, and then just as quickly turned back again, shaking his head. "Shit, almost forgot what I came to say. Keep an eye out for squatters. I run a whole group of them off last night bedded down in the lower forty, some religious folk carrying on like that were waitin' on somebody. Hell, the second coming of Christ, for all I know. Manorites they call themselves."

"Mennonites," JT said.

"You know 'em?"

JT shook his head. "It's what they're called."

"Whatever. Run 'em off. Once they get a hold on your land, it's damn near impossible to move 'em. Worse to get rid of than those wetbacked niggers."

JT's jaw tightened and he looked up at the sun.

"I say something that bothers you boy?"

"Sir?"

"You a nigger lover?"

"Don't much feel one way or the other."

"Those would be the choices."

They faced each other across the fence line.

"I'll keep an eye out for 'em," JT said.

The man turned his head and spat again, then studied JT a few minutes longer.

"I'm beginning to understand the short stick," he said. Then he pressed his boots to the sides of the horse and rode off.

B ox Canyon lay at the northwest corner of Gila Forest, massive limestone cliff walls that shielded the ruins of an abandoned stone mine. Keep Out signs were posted in now overgrown rocky vegetation and weathered by the elements amongst small mountains of graveled quartz and rhyolite scattered across the canyon floor, some tampered with by passersby or scavenging animals. The air was dry and hot and smelled of earthed stone from the bowels of the mine.

The horse pawed at the ground and shifted her feet, snorting. JT studied her movements, watching her ears stiffen, her head swing behind. He looked out over the canyon floor, but there was no life or soul about the place. A large piece of rusted drilling equipment sat behind them, blocking the mouth of the mineshaft. In the distance a kettle of vultures circled.

"Something out there, girl?"

He swung down from the saddle and stroked the horse's neck, then leaned down and breathed into her nostrils with his nose, talking in a calm, even voice, a technique he learned from Granddad. He pulled the lead rope with him, coaxing the horse's head down. Chica snorted and looked back again, then lowered her head. He continued to speak softly in her ear while he took hold of the bridle and walked the horse backwards down a gradual incline until the end of the travois was at the feet of a pile of granite. Then he retrieved the shovel from the litter. He had left the other equipment at the fence line to make room for the rock.

The shovel dug into the pile of rock and came away with pea-sized to small pieces of stone as JT lifted its weight and pitched it in the travois. The rocks made a clapping sound as they came together on the tarp and a cloud of dust rose above the heap. After he half-filled the travois, he bent down and scooped an extra shovel load in case he ran into the same situation with another post further down the line. The fourth load looked about right. JT tossed the shovel atop, then removed his blanket from the saddlebag and lay it across the end of the travois to stem the loss of moving rocks. With the back of his sleeve he pushed back his hat and wiped his brow, staring at the skeleton of a minecart resting on the remains of the laid down track leading into the mine. The canyon's walls trapped the sun's heat and soaked sweat from his skin. He untied the canteen from the saddle, unscrewed the cap and drank. He poured water into the well of his hat and held it out to the horse. She snorted and dipped her head, lapping at the water.

"We best get on."

Holding onto the bridle he moved her forward up the incline at an easy pace. When they reached level ground, the ricochet of a gunshot rang out. The echo exploded off the canyon walls in the emptied hush of the deserted quarry. JT grabbed hold of the reins as the horse reared.

"Whoa, girl."

It came from behind. He did his best to settle the horse, then tied the reins to a rusted spoked wheel half-buried in the dirt. He drew his gun and moved down into the canyon, flattening himself against the walls of rock. The remains of an old stone well lay in front of him and beyond that the opening of the mine. He lay against the rock wall, slowing his breathing, then made a dash to the well, half-expecting a flurry of gunfire to follow him. Not a sound. He crouched against the well wall and scanned the canyon for signs of movement. Not a breeze stirred. He guessed that whoever had fired the shot was holed up in the mine. He lay back against the stone and checked his gun—four bullets. He reached into his pocket and pulled out two more to fill the empty chambers. Then he closed the cylinder and rolled it. As he got to his knees and prepared to move, he heard the unmistakable click of a hammer dropping into an empty chamber. A puzzled look crossed his face. Slowly he stood and peered over the lip of the 20-ft well.

"Damn."

He found the squatters where the man said they'd be, still in the lower forty but now east of the fence line on Paraíso land, their wagon moored in the brush in an otherwise dry basin that checked a slow dribbling stream. It was suppertime when he came upon them, the sun still heavy on fire in the sky. Singing reached his ears, the thin strands of a young girl's voice stretched to reach the high notes of a hymn. The melody was choral, the voice pure and a relaxed peace fell over him, so immediate that he let out a deep breath and slowed the horse to a walk. A young boy's alto accompanied the girl's harmony and the deep baritone of an older man's voice joined in. The smell of roasted meat and boiled potatoes hung in the air and as he neared, the halo surrounding the fire seem to widen. *This must be what home feels like.*

The singing broke off when the horse and rider came into view.

"Don't stop on my account," JT said.

Three faces stared at him. A girl about 10 years old, a boy a few years younger, and a bearded man who wore a set of wire rimmed spectacles. All were dressed in black. They sat at a camped fire set a few yards from the wagon.

"Good evening," the man said. He stood and rested his left hand on a walking stick, the other held a leather-bound book.

"Howdy."

The girl's mouth formed a perfect "O," and she looked to her father who smiled reassuringly, then made a shooing motion with his right hand. She left the campfire and disappeared inside the wagon. The young boy stood next to his father.

"Do you own this land?" the man asked.

"No sir. I work for the man who does." He swung down from the horse. "But that's not why—"

"Vadder?" A young woman stepped out of the wagon. She looked at JT, then to her father.

"Es ist alles gut," the man said. His accent was thick and clipped.

The girl looked again at JT. Her eyes were the blue patter of rain and her hair the color of honey. She wore a simple black cotton dress with a high collar that trailed mid-calf, sashed at the waist from behind. The sleeves covered her arms, down to her wrists and the summer's heat produced a faint flush across her face, outlining the curves in her cheeks. Her hair flowed down her back from under the plain cap of white cotton on her head, the ends untied and trailing along the sides of her neck down the curves of the bodice. Loose strands of blond hair framed her face, while the black of the dress defined the clear whiteness of her skin. Had she been dressed in white, he would have sworn she descended from heaven. JT was wholly absorbed in looking at her, so much so that when her father cleared his throat it was JT's turn to flush.

"Gehen," her father said, this time sharply. The girl retreated into the wagon. He turned to JT and smiled, but his eyes remained serious. "We want no trouble."

"Yessir."

"We have no valuables and little money."

JT studied the man. He noticed the shadows under his eyes, the lines creasing his forehead. Dark circles stained his shirt, under his arms. The fire popped, heat reaching the small pockets of sap inside the wood's bark.

"What? No, I—"

"We will go by morning."

The young boy at his side pulled on his father's trousers.

"Aber, vadder ..."

"Jakob, schweigen."

"... wir können nicht ohne Peter."

"Schweigen!"

The man put his arm protectively around the boy, but Jakob broke free and ran to JT.

"Wir können nicht zu verlassen."

"Jakob!" The man chased after him.

"Mei bruder," he said to JT. His small fist pounded against JT's thigh. Then in English, "My brother."

The man stepped in and grabbed hold of him. The boy tried to wrench free, but his father held tight. Words flew between them in a foreign tongue until the boy broke down and cried, leaning into his father and burying his head in his chest. The father hugged him close, then bent and kissed him on the head. He spoke very soft. "Gott ist unser Hirte."

They stood that way for a breath of time, paired together as one. Then the man lifted his head.

"I apologize for my son's behavior. He misses his brother, you see. He misses ..." the man's words trailed off while his voice, strained and strangely quiet, finished the sentence, "...*Peter*." His arms slackened around the crying child and the boy looked up and followed his father's gaze. There, against the stranger's horse, holding tight to the litter pole stood Jakob's brother Peter. The raised voices had woken him and while they quarreled he had climbed from the travois. He stood before them, dirty and pale on shaky legs, a bandage wrapped around his calf.

"Peter!" Jakob ran to his brother.

The father stood dumbfounded and gazed upon his son as though witness to a holy act, Lazarus rising from the dead. Tears formed in the corners of his eyes. JT watched the folds in his appearance slacken and smooth, leaving his face bare and vulnerable. He turned to JT, but was quickly drawn back to Peter, unable to take his eyes off of him.

"Mei Sohn," he said, barely above a whisper.

"Mammi," Jakob shouted.

Jakob's mother and two sisters ran from the wagon and collectively they embraced the weary boy, huddled around him, wanting proof for themselves that it really was him, that he had, indeed, returned to them. The father moved closer and his large hands squeezed his wife's shoulder and that of his eldest son. Kissing, hugging and crying commenced, all at the same time.

JT moved off to allow them their privacy, hearing the fear in their voices surrender to relief, exhaling despair and replacing it with joy. He felt detached, witness to a moment in time that he would remember—and search for—the rest of his life. *This* is *what home feels like.*

P eter was pitching rocks in the stone well at Box Canyon Quarry when he heard the chink of stone hitting metal. The sun's light lit directly over the hole, and he could see the gun barrel peeking out from a pile of dead leaves scattered on the dry bottom.

"I sent you to collect wood. Why the quarry?" His father was seated around the fire with the rest of the family listening to Peter talk.

Peter shrugged. "Ich langweilte."

"Bored?" The father studied him, as though the words made no sense. "Where is it written that life must entertain you?"

The boy did not answer.

"Fortsetzen, go on."

He removed the rope tied to his saddle and wound it around a large stone about twenty feet away, then carried it to the well and dropped it in. It arrived two feet short of the well floor. He climbed over the rubbled lip and pulled hard, gauging the strength of his knot, then held tight while he lowered himself into the hole.

"Der Knoten. Hat es sich lösen?" Jakob asked.

The father turned to JT. "He wants to know if the knot came loose."

"Nein," Peter scolded, "sich gedulden."

His father laughed. "Since never has your brother had patience."

The deeper he descended, the stronger the smell of earth. When his left foot touched bottom, he stumbled on the scattered rocks he had tossed in and lost his balance. He let go of the rope and grabbed hold of the walls to steady himself. At the same time the heel of his right foot came down on the gun's trigger and it went off. The bullet ricocheted off the stone walls and badly nicked the side of his leg.

Peter threw off the blanket and pulled back the bandage on his leg to show his family the hole. The bullet had left a nick about the size of a dime that had scabbed over with blackened blood, the skin around it raised and pulling at the skin as it healed. His mother drew in breath and quickly covered him with the blanket again.

"Es ist zu heiß," Peter said.

"Leave it," his father said. "Finish your story."

When the bullet nicked his leg, blood immediately sprang up from the hole in his pants and he gripped it hard, howling in agony. His screams echoed up the well walls and spooked his horse. It took off running directly across the rope hanging between the well and the rock, pulling the rope with it. By the time he looked up only the end of the rope was visible at the mouth of the well.

The boy paused and looked at his father. "Es tut mir leid Vater. Ich verlor das Pferd."

Jakob shook his head. "Das Pferd ist hier."

Peter looked to his father. "Ja? Er ist hier?"

"Ja," his father said, "the horse is here. He made his way back."

This brought a smile to Peter's face and a sigh of relief.

"Beenden Sie die Geschichte," Anna said.

"Ja, finish the story" his father said.

To curb the flow of blood he unthreaded the belt from his pants and with hands trembling wrapped it around his thigh, took a deep breath and pulled. Tight. The pain was white and made him lightheaded. He slid to the floor of the well. *You're not going to die you're not going to die you're not going to die.* Sleep came while he repeated it. When he awoke hours later, the bleeding had stopped. But when he tried to stand the pain felled him, and he slid back to the bottom. The next four days were the longest of his life, endless hours calling for help until the rawness in his throat made him mute. The nights were cool and twice some animal came to the top of the well and growled, sniffing the soiled blood and sweat, trying to get at what the vultures knew was dying.

Many hours during the daylight he spent staring at the rope at the top of well, willing it to descend, once or twice hallucinating that it did. By then he knew it wasn't the wound that would kill him—it had scabbed over and miraculously showed no signs of infection. It was being buried alive in a tomb of stone. Each hour that passed took with it hope that deliverance would come. He wept when he thought about his family and how he would never see them again, and how they would never know the truth. They would think he simply ran away.

"Nein," Jakob said. "Nie."

Peter smiled weakly and rubbed his eyes.

During the daylight hours he used the tips of several rocks to scrawl a message on the inside of the well. "Ich liebe meine familie." Then below that, "Peter Friesen."

Marike and Anna reached for each other's hands and squeezed.

"Then what happened?"

Nothing. Nothing happened. He fell asleep, waited, fell asleep, and waited. Thirst overran his thoughts, so powerful that when he slept, he dreamed he was drowning. Each sunrise seemed to grow dimmer and each night longer than the one before. On the fourth day he surrendered. No one would find him. Not alive. That's when he picked up the gun and studied it, wondering why he had to have it. One bullet remained in the chamber.

Peter stopped talking and looked down at his feet. With the blanket over his shoulders, he looked like a misshapen dwarf hunched over the fire. Jakob opened his mouth to prompt him, but his father held up his hand. They would wait until Peter was ready, until he could regain the courage to speak the words he needed to say.

"I thought…," then in German, "ich dachte…", he hesitated, but the father would allow no one to speak.

Peter placed his hands on the sides of his head. "I thought I would use that bullet..." his voice trailed off.

"Es eine Sünde," Jakob blurted out. "Es nicht?" Twigs snapped as the fire flamed. The faces around the campfire turned to the father who gravely considered the matter and sighed.

"Jakob is correct. It is a sin. The time of our death is not of our choosing. Our lives belong to God and we have no right to end them. It is lack of faith which leads us to a loss of salvation."

The children murmured assent and looked at Peter.

"I shot the bullet into the air," Peter said, "so I would not be tempted."

"Then what happened?" his mother asked.

Peter looked first at his mother, then at each member of his family before turning toward JT.

"A miracle," Peter said.

JT sat with the family around the fire. He mopped up the gravy on his plate with biscuits Mrs. Friesen served him for supper. It had been a long time since he had tasted food that wasn't tortillas. He had heard Peter's story once before so was only half listening. It took him a moment to realize all talking had ceased. When he looked up from his plate, six pairs of eyes stared at him.

"Wait. Look," said JT, "it was pure coincidence I happened to be in the quarry—"

"—at the precise time—" the father said.

"—the shot was fired." Peter finished.

It was true that ten minutes before or after that moment would have put him on the other side of the canyon walls and outside of hearing the gunshot.

"Eine engel," Mrs. Friesen said.

JT laughed and put his plate down. He pushed back his hat. "I've been called many things in my life, ma'am, but angel ain't one of them."

"And this gun," the father asked his son, "the one you had to have?"

Peter pulled the revolver from the waistband of his pants. He held it up so they could see. The firelight on the barrel gave the metal a sheen. They stared at the instrument of his near demise.

"You know what to do," said his father.

Peter's face fell. "Aber, vadder—"

"Nein," the man said.

Peter stared at the gun for a moment longer, then held it out to JT.

"I can't take it," JT said.

"Bitte," the father said, "you must."

JT looked from Peter to the man, then back at Peter.

"Here's the thing," JT said. "I don't have room for it now. I've still got a few hundred acres I've got to cover."

Peter's face looked hopeful, but JT could see the father would not yield. He turned to Peter.

"How about you keep it for me, and when I get finished what I need to do, I'll come get it."

"In Mexico?"

"I imagine I'll get down that way before I die."

Peter's face broke into a grin. "Vadder?"

The father looked at JT, then nodded and smiled. "You are welcome in our home at any time."

That night JT dreamed he was broken on the floor of a dry creek, a thunderstorm above, methodically filling the creek with water. Rain splashed his eyes until they were covered and the breath escaping him made bubbles that floated above his soon-to-be watery grave.

He woke to find the night passed and the campsite empty. A bundle lay on the ground next to feet with food that Peter's mother had prepared. Underneath the tied string was a handwritten note, thanking him for his kindness and an address: Palomas, Mexico.

9.

The horse knew it before he did. There must have been a shift in the air, a down current that contained in it the burden of catastrophe, and she smelled it. She drew it in and listened to its counsel in the not-so-subtle way a horse's senses can prophesy misfortune when it arrives before the messenger.

He had been gone five days, five miserable days fixing fences and was headed back. They weren't but two miles from their destination when the animal he was riding came to a complete stop, lifted her head sideways and strained against the reins. He urged her forward but she pranced in the dirt, ears back, twisting sideways into a circle. As he reined her around, she whinnied and jerked her head, chewing at the side of the bit then pulled him into another circle, then back to the front. JT pushed her forward but she stalled, stopping and starting and tossing her head back. For a moment he feared she might rear.

"Whoa … easy. What is it girl?"

Chica remained tense, her nostrils widening, ears back. He flat out didn't know what she was trying to tell him.

"Whoa," he said, while she circled again. As they came full circle, he lifted his eyes and saw for himself the cause of her distress.

"Goddamn."

A swell of black smoke rolled upward into the sky, clouds of charcoal chasing it, spreading steadily higher. They lay thick and heavy against the heavens, a dark draped curtain. A coldness settled inside him. Nothing small-time was going to generate that kind of smoke, and he knew it. Holding tight to the reins, he dug his heels into the horse's flank and bore down into a gallop, leaning forward in the saddle to lengthen her stride, trying to cover the distance between himself and the Jackson ranch before his next heartbeat, and at the same time close the gap between himself and fate, knowing he didn't deserve the prayers he was praying under his breath, but knowing he needed them just the same. He struggled against giving into the panic just yet, not understanding why bad things happen to good people, and why the rest of the world is stuck in the middle watching.

In less than five minutes he crested the rise above the valley and reined the horse to a stop, her mouth foamed at the bit, the sweat soaked into her sides in dark patches. She snorted and reared as threads of smoke folded into them. He stared down into a bowl of blackness. From this distance he could see the stretch of the hacienda shrouded in black-grey, tiny flashes of red flame peeking through. JT could see the house was on fire, but how far it had spread and what other buildings were involved was beyond his view, so broad the haze of smoke.

"Shit. Come on."

He rode Chica into the valley towards the ranch, falling beneath the curtain of smoke, and still the air was thick with it. The horse struggled beneath him. He kept a stronghold on the reins and drove her forward down the slope of the land. Something in the speed at which they moved seemed to calm her. She resisted as they neared the house, engulfed in flames, a real live vision of hell on earth. He slid from the horse and stared at the wall of fire raging inside the house, its girth wide, consuming all dimensions of space within. The crackling of the splintered wood and the way the fire ate through it, its appetite voracious, its anger spilling into every crack and crevice through which the smallest sliver of air breathed. From the windows it spat and slapped against the now windowless squares cut into the wood, its fingers reaching forward, beneath the eaves of the veranda, licking the outer edges with an orange tongue. Flames cascaded upwards over the roof timbers. White wisped smoke danced ghost-like along the roof top as the wind buffeted the fire in different directions. He recognized the sharp smell of burnt lumber. JT turned back toward the horse, but she was gone.

He couldn't remember when he had seen a fire ablaze in all its glory like the one before him, and he stood, not knowing what to do. His mouth opened to call out, but before the words could form he knew in his heart that no living thing could be alive in the inferno burning before him. It was wall-to-wall flame. The bricks at the base of the house were blackened, its foundation crumbling under the fire's weight. Slowly he took off his hat and gripped it, all hope dwindling to a stone at the pit of his stomach. His knees lowered to the ground and he leaned back on his heels, staring upwards at the blaze, his awed expression reflected in its light. He remained there, mesmerized by the fire's beauty and by the futility of arriving at a place too late and too useless to do a damn thing. That's when he heard the horses.

The stables were at the south side of the hacienda, far removed from the house. He headed in that direction. The wind blew south and with it the smoke. He pushed through it, placing his hat against his face. Now and then he paused to cough and lean on his knees, trying to find clean air then pushed forward again. He could hear the horses, their whinnies carrying on the wind each time it shifted. No doubt the smoke had them panicked and rearing in their stalls. He thought of Pa and Harlan then moved on.

A fire in that kind of wind could burn a whole ranch to the ground without blinking an eye. He had seen its power in the gutted remains of a large spread in Tucumcari caught in a prairie fire. It took only two hours to scorch the place, reducing it to charred wood and ashes before dawn broke. The family escaped with breath in them but the same couldn't be said for their livelihood. That ranch was the only space between them and the road. It defeated old man Tucker, and he spent the rest of his life looking down the long neck of a bottle into an early grave.

Through the clouds of smoke he could see the outline of the stables against night's dusk. He was nearly to them when his foot caught on something heavy and solid and he went down, smacking his knee hard against the ground. He cursed and laid back to catch his breath, then turned to see what tripped him. It was Domingo. The Mexican lay in the dirt beside him, a bloody hole where the bullet entered right below the temple, powder singed into the man's skin. But he stopped staring at the bullet hole when he saw the scalping, how the blade had slid clean between hair and scalp, taking with it a layer of skin, exposing the top of Domingo's skull. JT vomited. Dragging the sleeve of his arm across his mouth, he lay back again, drawing in breath and clearing his throat. JT turned back toward Domingo and looked into the vacant stare of a dead man. Then the horses spoke to him again.

The fire hadn't reached the stables, so he knew they weren't in immediate danger. The smell of smoke had them frightened. He ducked inside and made his way to the first stall where Ruby stood trembling towards the back.

"Come on baby," he coaxed. She must have recognized his voice, because this time she came directly forward and he flattened himself against the stall door and let her pass. She broke into a lope and he watched her fly out into the night. Then he moved on to the next stall. Nothing in his life prepared him for what he found there.

The raw depravity of men's souls and the acts of which they are capable was made clear to JT the moment he opened the door. It was empty, save for the body of a woman who lay crumpled at the far back, abandoned like discarded trash. JT smelled whiskey and evil in that order. So sullied and mutilated was the body, scored with cuts and gashes and riddled in blood that caked in pools on her skin, that it wasn't until he was standing directly over her that JT realized it was Dalia's mother. Her blouse was ripped apart and her skirt was gone and the heels of her feet scored with several deep slash marks. They had ravaged her with teased knife marks along her breasts and thighs and left her legs cruelly twisted in an unnatural pose. He could see the wide gash in her throat, severed clean to the bone. It gaped open in a cruel grin. The space beneath her was soaked red, the sticky cooled thickness of the blood drawn from its now hollow space and lay heavy in the straw. She was still warm to the touch and held the same vacant stare he witnessed in Domingo, the way her eyes looked out into the world seeing nothing and everything at the same time, the light behind them gone from this earth forever and passed on into a place of knowing.

JT retrieved her shawl, discarded in the straw, knelt beside her and covered her nakedness as best he could. He passed his hands over her eyelids, drawing them down. He then passed a hand over his own eyes, feeling the moisture beneath his fingers and took a breath, holding it a moment longer than necessary, then letting it out slowly in the manner of a person who bears witness to the savageries of mankind rarely unveiled in the plainness of day and company of good men. The bile rose again in his throat, but this time he pushed it down.

Kneeling there he heard the faint thin sounds of weeping, carried in the open rafters of the stable.

"Dalia?"

He rose cautiously. Slowly he removed his gun from its holster, pulling the hammer back with painstaking slowness. He held it at the ready and took another deep breath. Then moving quickly, he travelled from one stall to the next, hurling each door open with strength bolstered by fear. When each door opened he made room for the horse to bolt, then quickly trained his gun inside. Empty. He moved to the next. Empty. Then the next and the next. Empty, empty. As he moved along the corridor, the weeping in the stable intensified. At the last stall he grabbed the handle and pulled, pointing his gun inside. A girl lay crouched at the very back, partially buried in the straw. She was alone. She screamed and cowered, raising her hands to cover her head. He re-holstered his gun and came to her, taking hold of her arms to pull them from her face. She flailed against him, screaming. In a soft voice he tried to calm her.

"Rosalía. It's me, JT."

The girl continued to wail. "No, no, no …"

"Rosalía …"

"No, no, no…."

"Rosalía. It's me. JT. You're safe. Salvo." He smoothed back the hair on her head and brought her face directly in front of his. "Rosalía. Escúchame. Es JT, JT, recuérdame?"

The girl paused her crying.

"JT?"

"Sí."

Rosalía's crying gave way to sobbing. He felt the weight of her shoulders as she buried her face against his chest.

"Rosalía. Escúchame. Dalia. ¿Donde esta?"

At the mention of Dalia's name the girl stopped sobbing. She lifted her eyes to his and gripped his arm.

"Dalia?" she said.

"Sí, sí. Dalia. Donde esta?"

"Ido."

"Gone? Gone where? ¿Dónde?"

Rosalía's eyes had a wild look to them.

"No sé," she said. She began to cry again.

He gripped her by the shoulders. "Piensa, think," he said, shaking her lightly, trying to draw her focus.

"No sé, no sé," she blubbered.

He gripped her tighter, turning her face towards his. "Me miras. Usted debe saber." *You must know.* He held her chin in his hand, forcing her to face him. She looked up at him. Her eyes widened and she screamed.

The butt of the gun hit him across the back of the head, and he fell into the straw. A boot kicked the side of his face. Another landed in his gut. He groaned and curled himself into a ball. He could hear Rosalía's cries, but they sounded far away.

"Careful boys," a man's voice said. "We don't want to kill him before we hang him."

10.

"I told you. I don't know him."

"Well, he says he knows you."

"He don't."

The sheriff sat with his hands folded in front of him, prayer-like, studying JT, trying to gauge the truth in his eyes. They occupied a room of the La Cruces Amador Hotel that doubled as an office when the sheriff had a need for it. The walls were papered in blue paisley print that had a dizzying effect if you stared at it too long. In the corner of the room was a double sized bed set in a wrought iron frame with pale blue chenille bedding to match the walls. In the middle of the room was a desk made of mahogany wood, too small for the lawman's legs to fit comfortably underneath, the strength of its grain lacquered many times over trying to hide its age. On top of the desk stood two water glasses, one for the sheriff and one for JT, which neither had touched. The man and the boy sat on either side of the desk, taking inventory of the other.

"Roy says you two go way back."

"That's a lie."

"I'd like to believe you son, I would. But without anyone to back the truth of what you're telling me, I can't let you go."

"What about the foreman?"

"Dead."

"What about Mr. Jackson?"

"Dead."

"What about—"

"They're all dead, son."

Outside in the street were the faint sounds of men talking. JT heard the sound of a can being kicked and the bray of a donkey in the distance. He hated to ask the question weighing on his mind.

"What about his daughter?"

"You tell me."

JT gave the sheriff a hard look. The sheriff met his look and leaned back in his chair. Outside the sound of hooves accompanied by wagon wheels approached then moved away. Finally the sheriff sighed and leaned forward.

"Look son. I know I shouldn't be telling you this, but here's the thing. I like you." He paused a moment and looked at JT. "The way I understand it, Dalia Jackson ran off two days before this happened. It took her Pa a day to find out she was missing. He was fixin' a posse to help find her when this hell rained down."

There was relief in that knowledge. Relief that she wasn't there, like the sheriff said, when the ranch went up in flames.

"Anyone looking for her?"

The sheriff dropped his eyes to his hands. "We're keeping an eye out, if that's what you mean."

"I mean, have you sent your deputies looking for her?"

"Look here, son. We don't have the manpower to chase down runaways. Shit, we barely have enough men to deal with what we're dealing with now. For all we know she could be holed up with some trail hand not wanting to be found."

"That's not how it would be."

"Then why don't you tell me how it would be?"

JT looked to his hands then back up at the sheriff. "She'd want to know. She'd want to know what happened to her family."

"I can appreciate that. I can. But it's not my job to be tracking down people to tell them about their kin. I got my hands full here. And for starters, I need to get to the truth."

"What about Rosalía? She knows who I am."

"We already talked to her."

"And?"

"And she says you were there."

"What?"

"She says you were there that night."

"Of course I was there. I found her. Right when you found me."

"Sometimes she says you were there lighting fires, and sometimes she says no. Can't tell us much more than that. She's a bit shook up."

JT stared at the paisley print on the wall.

"Look. If what you're saying is the truth, and I'm not saying it is," the sheriff said, "you were mighty lucky to be gone when you were. Otherwise we'd be counting you among the soon to be buried. If what you say is true. Yessir, mighty lucky." He drew out the last part slow, watching JT as he said it.

"The truth ain't got but one story," JT said.

The lawman studied his face for a breath of time, looking from one eye to the other. Then he leaned back in his chair again. Outside a donkey brayed.

"You know I have a son just about your age and I'd hate to see him mixed up in this kind of business. I understand your pa's passed on. And your brother too."

JT sat up straight. "Then you know where I come from and how this ain't who I am."

"Hell, that's don't tell me nothing. When a fella loses everything and everyone he cares about in one fell swoop, well, sometimes that kinda gives him the idea like he's got nothing more to lose. It makes for some wild ideas running 'round his head."

"It don't make me a murderer."

"No, I reckon it don't. That'd take quite a leap." The sheriff sighed. "But I've seen it, boy. I've seen the most god fearin' people turn a blind eye to killin' down here quicker than you can spit. It takes over their life. They fancy themselves a real live Jesse James, thinking they're going to get revenge on the world for the way life's treated them. That wouldn't be you, would it?"

"No sir. It ain't."

The sheriff studied him. "Scalpings are ugly business. Looks like some Indians may have been involved."

"I don't see it that way."

"Why's that?"

"Indians believe a man's soul is in his scalp. It's like a prize, a—

"—trophy."

"That's right. A trophy. They wouldn't have left it behind. I don't know about the rest, but Domingo's scalp was laying not five feet from him."

"So what are you sayin'? Are you telling me they tried to make it look like Indians were involved?"

"I'm just saying, it's not an Indian's nature to leave the prize behind."

"Is that so?"

"Yessir, I believe so." JT studied the sheriff. "But then, you already knew that, didn't you sir?"

The sheriff met the boy's gaze.

"I reckon I did," said the sheriff. "I reckon I did." He picked up one of the water glasses and drank from it.

He looked at JT and pointed to the other glass. JT shook his head.

"Suit yourself." The sheriff took another deep swallow and placed the empty glass back on the desk.

"Let's talk about you and Roy. According to him, you two met back up on the plains about a week ago."

"It weren't no week."

"So then he's telling the truth."

JT raised his cuffed wrists and rested them on his head. Then he dropped them in his lap. He looked at the sheriff.

"I told you. I don't know him. He made camp with me one night a couple weeks ago, that's all. Never saw him before that night. I swear that's the truth."

"Never before."

"Never."

"So he's lying."

"Yessir, he is."

The sheriff took a moment to study the boy again, taking note of how often he met his gaze straight on without dropping his eyes.

"He sure knows a lot about you for someone you just met once."

"Like what?"

"Like that you hail from Clayton, New Mexico. Like your name don't stand for nothing but JT. That you pack a twelve-gauge shotgun and a Colt .45 and that you're headed to California."

"That's not a whole lot of information you can't get when you're sharing a meal together over a fire."

"It's a whole lot more information than I'd be disclosing to a stranger. Information you can't dispute is the truth. And since you can't give me nothing to hang a nail on to the contrary, I can't help but wonder who's lying. You or ol' Roy.

"Like I said. There ain't but one truth."

"And you're telling it."

"Yessir I am."

"And how do I know you're not lying?"

"I reckon you don't."

The clock on the wall ticked loudly.

There was a light rap on the hotel room door. It opened and the deputy stepped through. He bent down and whispered into the sheriff's ear with his head turned from JT. The sheriff listened and nodded.

"Uh-huh. Of course I know him," the sheriff said.

While he listened, the sheriff looked at JT.

"Okay, thanks Ben." The deputy stepped out of the room and the sheriff turned to JT.

"Well son, looks like this is your lucky day." He stood up from his chair and stretched his legs.

"You found Dalia Jackson?"

The sheriff stopped and stared at JT. "No. That's not—No, I mean, we're cutting you loose." He fingered the key chain on his belt and moved towards JT's side of the desk.

"Sir?"

"Why didn't you mention the fact that you ran into Warren Murray while you was fixing those fences?"

"Who?"

"You didn't think that was important information?"

"I spoke some to a stranger, but I didn't get his name."

"Well, that stranger just happens to be Warren Murray, and he owns the farm bordering Jackson's ranch. Warren heard about the fire and came into town to find out what happened. That's when he found out about you. He told us he met you two days ago out on Jackson's spread fixing fences."

JT held out his arms as the sheriff bent over him and inserted the key into the lock. There was a soft click and the handcuffs opened.

"I think you just might have a guardian angel watching over you boy. Just might."

JT rubbed his wrists. "Excuse me sir, but how do you know this Warren fella ain't lying?"

The sheriff smiled. "Warren? Naw. He and I go way back. He's all leather. No, anything Warren Murray has to say out is the truth; you can take that to the bank. He's done gifted you an alibi—couldn't have picked a finer upstanding citizen for the job. You're free to go son."

JT looked to the water on the desk and the sheriff nodded, handing him the glass. He drank quickly. The sheriff held out his hand and JT shook it.

"I don't mind telling you," the sheriff said, "I'm glad things worked out the way they did. If Warren had showed up one day later, well, you'd be on your way to Albuquerque for a trial and possibly a hanging. And I hate to say it, but these days, not necessarily in that order."

When light broke in the dark of the following day, JT was sixty miles north of Las Cruces. He had ridden all night and not stopped until he reached Caballo Lake. The sun's grace set down on the water like the glistening of some newly made miracle, the reverent awakening of the world. There he stopped and watered Ruby. He loosened her cinch and talked to her softly, apologizing for the demands he made upon her over the course of the night and the stretch of land they covered. A light dampness tamped the land. Over the lake, fog burned off in the early morning heat. A horde of snow geese rose from the water, their white wings dark against the redness of the sun's rising. The horse was plenty tired, but they still had far to go.

They weren't there more than an hour before he saw riders approaching in the distance. Two men on horseback, the one in the lead packing a rifle. Shadowed against the dawn's approach he could see the rope that connected the two—the horse behind tethered to the one in front.

When the men were a quarter mile out, he tightened Ruby's cinch and swung himself back up into the saddle. He put her forward, positioning himself in the depression of a narrow swale swallowed up in a stand of creosote bush. As soon as the riders passed, he and the horse stepped up and into the road behind them. Aiming the rifle at the backs of the riders, he cocked the gun, the hard tinny click loud enough to fill the space of still air between the three horsemen. The riders immediately stopped. The one in the lead slowly turned to face him, his hand raised in the air.

"I just want him," JT said. He nodded the rifle in Roy's direction.

The deputy lowered his hands when he recognized the boy pointing the rifle. He looked to his own rifle, holstered in the gear on his horse's saddle.

"I've got orders to take this man to Albuquerque to stand trial for murder."

"I know it. I've just got different plans, that's all."

The deputy's eyes drifted to his rifle, then back to the boy.

"Son, you don't want to be doing this."

"I don't see I have much of a choice."

"What's that mean?"

"It means I need you to dismount your horse, sir. Easy."

The deputy stared at the boy but didn't move. "It's a federal offense—"

JT pulled back the hammer. The deputy stopped talking. He dismounted his horse slowly, lowering himself to the ground.

"Keep your hands where I can see them and move away from the horse."

The deputy raised his hands and took a number of steps back, his eyes flicking from the boy to the rifle holstered on his own horse, then back at the boy. JT pushed Ruby forward alongside the deputy's horse and grabbed the reins.

"The town of Hatch is about 20 miles thataway," JT said, jerking his thumb south. "If you start now, there's a good chance you can get there before nightfall."

JT untied the canteen from the deputy's horse and threw it to him. He pressed his boots to Ruby's side and headed out, trailing Roy and his horse behind, kicking up a cloud of dust in their wake. He glanced behind and saw the deputy pull a pistol from his boot. He urged Ruby into a run just as two shots fired from the deputy's pistol. When the dust cleared, the riders were gone.

11.

They rode all day and into the night. JT ignored Roy's calls to stop, paying out the rope to create a deeper distance between the horses. They passed over small streams and JT slowed to let the horses drink, ignoring Roy's cries of thirst. As Roy's luck would have it, an hour later the heavens opened and pummeled them in the form of a sun shower that lasted a good fifteen minutes. The moisture felt good on their sun baked skin and Roy opened his mouth to catch the rain, his cracked lips numb to their touch. In the very early hours of the following day they reached the foothills of the Florida Mountain wilderness and by the full moon's light trailed a dried-out arroyo where they picked their way through the sandstone and scrub brush until they reached an abandoned mine, sixty miles west of Las Cruces. Men and horses were played out. A few feet from the mine lay a stone stock tank, crippled by unuse. It held a shallowness of water, half full.

JT slid from the saddle and dropped the reins. He unpacked his canteen and headed toward the tank, a pounding in his head making his eyes water. He pulled the bandana from his forehead and it came away stiff, crusted with blood. The deputy's bullet had sliced into the skin above his right eye just below the hairline and opened a gash that had poured forth, its sticky wetness now caked on his skin. His fingers touched the wound, knew it was deep. He drank then dunked his head fully into the cool sweetness of the water.

He whistled to Ruby and she came to the water, blew at it and drank. JT picked up the rope anchoring the two horses and pulled, coiling it into a loop as he collected it. When the horses were a few feet apart, he looped the rope around Ruby's saddle horn. Roy's voice had grown hoarse over the course of the ride, yelling at JT to stop, that he was thirsty, and where were they going anyway. As JT approached, Roy opened his eyes, weary and dust caked. JT reached up and took hold of the chain between the handcuffs and in a deliberate jerk, yanked him down from the horse. Roy hit the ground hard, nothing to break his fall.

"Shit. What the fuck was that?" Roy rolled facing him, trying to spit, but the dryness in his mouth resisted.

"That's for the lies you told the sheriff." JT turned the canteen upside down and water washed into Roy's face. His mouth opened to catch the last drops before it emptied. He turned his head and spat, then looked at JT.

"I reckon I had that coming," Roy said. His manacled hands rubbed the right side of his head where he had fallen. Then he levered his elbows, pushing himself to his knees and sat back on his haunches, still spitting dirt from his mouth. "Damn."

"Get up," JT said.

Roy rolled back on his heels, then made to stand. JT hit him across his jaw. Roy went down again, the manacles slicing into his wrists. He spit out blood.

"What the—?"

"That was for Dalia's mother. Make your peace cabrón, you're going to die."

"Now hold on there cowboy. I know you're looking for a dog to kick, but it ain't me. I didn't know they was fixing to do that. I swear. It's them crazy Mexicans."

"What Mexicans?"

"Some boys I hooked up with. We were supposed to loot the place, not kill nobody, I swear. I don't know what happened. Them boys were soaked on Indian whiskey. Things jus' got out of hand." Roy wiped the blood from his mouth with the back of his hand.

"You lying sack of shit. When I'm done with you, there'll be nothing left for the vultures, you sorry sonofabitch. Getup."

The calmness with which JT harnessed his anger scared Roy. Stirrings of real fear showed in his face.

"Get up, I said. Get. Up."

"Now hold on there, JT," Roy said, bringing himself to a kneeling position. "You gotta think this thing through."

"Shut up and get up."

"No, I mean it. You gotta think about how you're gonna find her. That's what you're after, ain't it? If you do something stupid like killing me, you'll never—"

JT slammed his fist against Roy's head. He went down again.

"Fuck!"

"Where is she?"

Roy lay on the ground, breathing heavy. Blood ran down the side of his mouth.

"That's what I'm trying to tell you. That's how this all got started. We met her outside of Canutillo.

"Bullshit." JT drew back his fist but Roy held up his hands to ward off the blow, the chain between his hands stretched tight.

"It's the truth, I swear it."

"What makes you think I'm fool enough to believe you?"

"What choice you got?"

JT walked to Ruby and unholstered his gun. He returned, checking the barrel before closing it. "There's always a choice," JT said.

"Hold on, hold on. Don't go doing something stupid."

"Only stupid being done is listening to your bullshit. You're gonna tell me the whole goddamn truth and it better wash. This Colt is itching to put you out of my misery."

At the entrance to the mine JT made a fire with gathered scrub brush and fanned the flames with his hat, then piled on more wood. He hobbled the horses and set them out to graze at the meager vegetation in the outcropping area. The animals turned to watch embers of fire spiral up into the black heavens, then distractedly resumed their grazing. JT trussed Roy to a large boulder, the rope pulled tight across his chest, making Roy howl. From his saddlebag he pulled the cornbread and beans with bacon and tortillas bizcochos he had purchased before leaving town. He made coffee in tin cups from the water in the tank and set over the fire to heat. The ache in his head had calmed to a dull throb and he felt along the edges of the bullet wound, sore to the touch.

"He singed you good," Roy said. "That's a nasty cut." He watched JT's hand jump back as it touched the gash. "I can sew that if you—

"Shut up. Talk."

The story Roy told held water. He and his band of Mexicans had crossed paths with Dalia outside of Canutillo, Texas, in the border town of Three Hills three days before the fire at the ranch. Roy had thrown in with the Mexicans looking to make some fast cash smuggling a group of illegals over the border. They had dumped their cargo in the desert outside of El Paso and were headed back when they ran into her. They didn't know where she was headed, only that it was south. She wouldn't give up much. She had kept close to the mountain range at the foot of Bear Ridge, most likely trying to keep out of sight.

"She's lucky I was there."

"How's that?"

"Those Mexicans. They was planning on doing some sick things."

"And you put a stop to it."

"I did."

"Expect me to believe that?" JT asked.

"Believe what you want cowboy, but the fact is, we wouldn't be having this conversation if it had ended where it had started. I've done a lot of things I'm not proud of, but none of it's got to do with harming women."

"But you throw in with men that do."

Roy looked down at his manacled hands.

"Go on," JT said. "How'd you stop them?"

"I got the idea to ransom her."

"Say what?"

"Ransom her. I recognized her name. I knew her daddy owned the Paraíso Ranch in Cruces. I convinced those Mexicans there was bigger money to be had than schlepping those wetbacks across the border. Nothing talks like gold."

JT gave him an ugly look, "Keep on. Why didn't you ransom her?"

"We were gonna, that was the plan. But when we got to the ranch ..." Roy looked down at his hands again.

"What?"

Roy shook his head. "I dunno. Like I said, things jus' got out of hand."

"How?"

"I dunno. The Mexicans, they were sauced, and we was expecting the pa to come to the door, you know, so we could do business."

"Do business."

"Yeah. I know how it sounds."

JT stopped playing with the stick and stared at the man across from him. Roy looked away. "But *she* came to the door," JT said.

"Yeah. Hell yeah, the wife came to the door. And those Mexicans, well, you can see where Dalia gets her looks."

"Shut up," JT said.

"I didn't mean nothin' disrespectful by it," Roy said, lifting his hands to shield his face.

"Go on."

"It's like you said. She came to the door and those Mexicans, well, before I had a chance to speak, they tried to lay their hands on her and she starts to scream, then the husband come up behind her with a gun and all hell broke loose. That's how I got this." He pulled up the leg of his pants to reveal a bandage that straddled the bottom of his left thigh.

"Jackson shot you?"

"Clean through my left leg. Knocked me down."

"And Jackson?"

"Them Mexicans blasted him every which way to Sunday."

A dry silence settled. Nothing in the desert moved, not a single shooting star overhead and nothing skittered in the creosote brush that scaled the mountains. It was barren and dark and echo-like quiet.

"Then what?"

"Shit. I don't know. I could hardly walk. I dragged myself off the porch and made it to the bunkhouse. Must have passed out, 'cause I don't remember anything until the sheriff woke me. Then he dragged me into the barn to show me their handiwork." Roy dropped his head.

"Go on."

"That's it."

"Can't be."

"That's it, I swear. That's all I know."

"Where is she?"

"Dalia? We left her tied up in a cave on Squaw Mountain. She didn't see none of it."

Another silence. JT threw the stick into the fire and stood.

"That's all I know, I swear," Roy said.

"If that's the case, I won't be needing you now, will I?" JT stood and rested his hand on his pistol.

"Now hold on JT."

"Where is she?"

"I ain't out to harm the girl.

"Where is she?"

"You're not gonna like it."

"Shit, I ain't liked nothing you've said. Where's she at?"

"They talked about selling her. Before we came up with the plan to ransom." Roy looked up at JT, his face fixed in a stare. "I told you, you weren't gonna like it."

"Where?"

"I don't know."

"Where?"

"One of those whore houses down in Juárez I expect."

"You sonofabitch."

"There weren't nothing I could do. I swear."

"You worthless sack of shit."

"Now hold on cowboy—"

JT hit him hard across the jaw.

"Sonofabitch!"

How long?" JT said. His fist trembled.

Roy spit out a tooth and a mess of blood.

"How long?"

Roy massaged his jaw and wiped blood from his mouth. "I dunno. Right after they left the ranch I reckon. They'd figure people would be looking for her. This way they could get rid of her and make some money at the same time."

The throbbing in JT's head was back. He turned his head and spat. Then he walked out beyond the lights of the campfire and stood looking up at the stars, the way their power arced across the heavens and the way the night's silence spoke to him like thunder inside his head. The dark blue coolness of the universe poured over in thick waves. He felt a scream bubble up inside him but stifled it. A coyote howled a hundred yards out, its cry clear and sharp like the strings of a harp. He stared at the sky for a long time, envisioning all the mysteries of the universe contained there. Looking for the key. Then his gaze rested on the twinkling lights, spread out below him. Twenty miles from the border of Mexico and the blue glow of the cantinas shone in the distance like a carpet of jewels set down in the desert.

JT returned to the fire and Roy lay propped against the boulder half-asleep, trying to doze off. Roy looked up when a shadow draped him, a dark figure outlined in the moon's light.

"You're gonna take me there," JT said.

"Where?"

"Juárez."

"I told you, I don't know where—"

JT drew his gun and placed the muzzle directly in the middle of Roy's forehead.

"I ain't asking. I'm telling."

12.

They slept most of the next day. JT roused Roy from sleep an hour after the sun went down and in the dark they broke camp and headed out, knowing the horses couldn't be pushed. Roy resisted weakly. He cursed and spat, held onto the saddle horn with his manacled hands and hoisted himself onto his horse. JT did likewise and in a matter of minutes the arroyo sat deserted as if they never were.

As they left the mine the cacophonous sound of wings beating filled the air and the horsemen stopped. A funneled cloud of bats spiraled out of the mine's opening, rising silhouetted against the full moon, their swelled numbers casting shade over the already shadowed cordillera to the south.

Roy raised his arms to his head. "Shit, them's vampire bats."

"They're free tails, jackass," JT said.

The horses moved at a slow, even pace, feeling their way in the dark amongst the scree. They rode in silence, the blackness of the night sky blued by the peppering of stars that dotted the heavens. The air smelled sweet, not yet soiled by sweat or dust, its coolness welcomed. A rough path to the side of the foothills led them down into a broad flat arroyo at its base, and from there they followed a dry riverbed south. The riverbed crossed east into a river basin where they stopped and watered the horses at a tinaja sinkhole. Across State Highway 9 they paralleled an old railroad grade for about a mile before it diverged south into the foothills of Camel Mountain and climbed upward. As the landscape rose, and them with it, the horses picked their way through limestone and scrub brush, stepping slow but sure-footed along a narrow path carved in the side of the mountain grown rocky. JT loosened the rope around his saddle horn and paid out more slack before dallying it again. Off to the west the lights of Palomas glittered. To the south the border beckoned them as they approached, the quiet of the Mexican desert fanned out before them in blanketed darkness lit by the moon's reflection off the limestone monoliths rising from the earth like hunched beasts.

An hour later they descended the opposite side of the mountain where, at its bottom, stood an old ranchstead fallen into disrepair and abandoned. They crossed over a dirt county road, and in that same night's blackness they crossed the border, silent and without incident into Mexico, riding slowly side by side along the dusty road and stepping onto the mesa in the darkness of the Chihuahuan desert, each horse hoof against the gravel loud in the darkened silence, where the man-made line demarking the separation of countries gave false hope to the idea that the earth can be owned, not understanding the impossibility of owning the sky, or the pureness of water. Not understanding that the land has its own ideas about being owned and could not be tamed. It seemed the appetite of man had devoured this part of the earth and left behind only sand.

JT reined the horses to a stop and looked back from where they came. From where the whole of his life beckoned to him, everything he knew and had known. The land that had twisted and shaped him in ways he wouldn't have imagined. The land that tied him to his past yet allowed him a glimpse of his future before stealing it away, making him earn it. Asking him if he wanted it badly enough. Holding it barely out of reach with no promise that it would remain unchanged should he find it. He took off his hat and wiped his brow with the sleeve of his shirt, pain radiating as it passed the wound in his forehead. It made him think again of the events of his life threaded together and that all they contained were strands of a bigger web. All beasts share the air that gives first and last breath.

Then he turned back to the new country where he stood on the precipice of this new life and could not foresee the shape it was intent on fashioning for him now, nor the ways it would change him. He just knew it would. He took a deep breath of night's air that hadn't been soiled yet with the sweat of men and dust upturned by the sun's heat and a calmness overtook him. The horses too felt its peace, their breathing ordered and small puffs of white smoke trailing from their nostrils.

Far off to the southwest the Sierra Madres hung suspended in the dark. Both men stood the horses on the mesa and watched them, the clouds shifting in and out of the moon's light giving them the appearance of mountainous islands floating in the sky. The adjacent mountains were walled with trap rock and scoured with pock marked holes while below a withered creek sported a gravel bar overgrown with creosote and willow. A black footed ferret darted the desert grassland bar.

"Well. We done it," Roy said.

JT cupped his hand around a match and lit a cigarette. He passed it to Roy.

"I know it."

"Who would have guessed the two of us would have been crossing it together?" Roy said. He laughed and took a drag on the cigarette.

"Who would have guessed you'd still be alive."

They slept for two hours in a dry wash at the foot of the mesa. When JT woke, his head throbbed and the vision in his right eye was blurry. He unscrewed his canteen and poured water over his head. The cool liquid felt good against the heat of his skin. He kicked Roy. "Get up."

Roy turned and rubbed his eyes. The handcuffs had bruised his wrists, and he pushed them up to rub underneath. "That's a bad lookin' cut you got there," Roy said.

"Saddle up."

They rode slowly down into a broad swale bordered by ledges on either side, the sand beneath the horses dotted with scrub brush. The makings of a faint road was before them and off to the side sat a weathered signpost with the words "La Linea" carved in the wood.

"Sound familiar?"

"Hell, I've never been this far west crossing the border, cowboy. All I know is to head east. If they ain't left her for dead."

JT looked at him. Then he dismounted Ruby and walked towards Roy.

"I'm just stating the facts, that's all," said Roy. "What's she running from anyhows?"

JT said nothing. He cut a length of rope and knotted the chain of the handcuffs to the pommel, yanking it tight while Roy grimaced. Then he unloosed the rope connecting the two horses.

"Keep in sight or you're dead."

T he town of La Linea leaned into the mud-tilled earth the way a kicked dog leans into the shadows. To escape notice. A spattering of low houses with mud bricked walls, roofs of corrugated sheet iron in grooved curves spread out along the dusted path like discarded boxes, smelling of molded rust and ammonia. They were greeted with stares, ink black eyes of women, children, old men and young men who hung in the doorways or squatted on stools outside the houses. A handful of children rose from their squatting position looking into a hole in the ground and watched them ride past. In the doorways of the shacks young men, and some old, stood watching them, their mouths a straight line with rolled cigarettes between their lips. JT tipped his hat wordlessly, getting a vacant stare in response. The hooves of the horses hitting ground deafened the silence.

"This place is quieter than a Sunday," Roy said. He flinched when the caw of a crow broke the stillness and seeing his reaction the children laughed. "Shit. Quiet as a grave."

"Quit workin' your mouth and keep your eyes on the road."

They stopped at a mud tienda where JT dismounted and tied the horses to the post. As he entered the hut Roy called out to him.

"You just gonna leave me here?"

"You got company. I won't be long." The children had followed the strangers and now pressed close to Roy's horse, making it skitter.

"Por favor señor, por favor," they begged with hands outstretched. JT smiled as he heard Roy swear and yell, "Vámoose!"

In the store he bought coffee, a sack of oats for the horses, two tins of beans, tortillas and cheese. Behind the counter a woman clothed in a dark rebozo eyed him under thick eyelashes and lowered head while she rang up the purchase and surprised him when she spoke, her voice soft.

"Te gusta la leche?"

"¿Qué?"

"¿La leche de cabra?" She pointed to a small goat tied to a pole outside the back door.

He noticed the thinness of the woman's frame, the shadows under her eyes. A painted wood lamina hung on the far wall behind her, splintered, its colors faded. Underneath it lay a wizened dog, its muzzle white, its mouth open as it breathed.

"Sí, una copa." The milk was thickly puddled and as he raised it to his mouth a rank gamey smell made him hesitate before taking a deep breath and swallowing. He set down the cup.

"¿Más?"

"No, gracias. Por favor, ¿sabe usted qué tan lejos a Juárez?

The woman shook her head.

"Gracias señora." He collected his items and left the store, feeling the weight of the goat's milk in his stomach.

"It's about time," Roy said. "I'd about baked to a crisp in this sun."

JT handed Roy the canteen, then packed the tortillas, beans and cheese in his saddlebag. He poured a portion of the oats into his hat and held it out to Ruby and then to Roy's horse. He then placed the remainder in the saddlebag, untied the horses from the post and mounted.

"Any whiskey?" Roy asked.

JT ignored the question and threw two pesos to the children. While they ran from the horses and scrabbled on the hard dirt for the coins, he turned the horses back down the road they had entered. The doorways of the shacks they passed were empty now, the spectacle having passed, and they were nearly to the outskirts of town when a group of horsemen appeared from the opposite direction and blocked their path.

"Shit," Roy said under his breath.

"Let me talk," JT said as the riders approached.

There were five of them dressed in sweat stained, worn uniforms, remnants of a long-ago revolution, complete with hats and boots and buscadores, some harnessing government issued automatic pistols. Two of them had bandoliers strapped across their chests. As they milled in the road and faced each other, JT recognized one as the young man who leaned in the doorway when they had passed on their way into town.

"Hola," JT said.

After a few moments of silence, the middle rider leaned his head to the side and spat. "Son Americanos?" the rider said.

"Sí."

The rider nodded and looked beyond him towards the village, then back at him. His hands crossed loosely at the wrist.

"Quien es su prisionero?

"¿Qué?"

With a jerk of his chin he gestured towards Roy. "Su prisionero. Quien es?" While he spoke another rider rode up and halted beside Roy. With the butt of his rifle he raised Roy's hands to reveal the handcuffs.

"Es un ladron. Lo estoy retomar America."

¿Qué fue lo que robó?

JT stared back at them. "No es importante."

The other riders looked at each other and smiled. The man who had spoken did not. He had not taken his eyes from JT. The next time he spoke was in English.

"It is not for you to say what is and is not important." He leaned and spat again.

"Your papers."

"I have no papers."

"No documentos?"

"No."

The man studied him for a while.

"This is very bad."

Roy looked to JT, but JT had not taken his eyes off the Mexican. Ruby shifted underneath him.

"I must take the prisoner."

"And who are you?"

The Mexican smiled, revealing rotten teeth. "Soy el capitán Ramirez de los Mexican Federales."

"JT, you ain't going to leave me—"

"Capitán, this man is my charge. I am responsible for him."

"In this country I am responsible."

The Captain nodded and two horsemen moved forward on either side of Roy. One Mexican grabbed the reins while the other man kept his eyes trained on JT, resting his hand on the gun holstered in his belt.

"JT—" The timbre of Roy's voice rose.

"Where will you take him?"

"¿Qué?" the Capitan asked.

"¿A dónde lo llevan?

The Capitán smiled. "No es importante."

13.

I sleep with the palms of my hands facing up, reaching for something but can't remember what, waiting for a hand to be slipped inside in reassurance, and I dream that water is poured through them, my hands cupped to receive it, the unbearable feeling of life slipping through my fingers.

Who am I? I ask myself this each time I come alive again, a long, long time in awakening, bubbled up from the depths of a stilled darkness I have escaped to, my arms dead weights anchored to my sides, my lungs and internal organs sunk to the very bottom walls of my chest, each breath stirring awake the nerve endings in parts of my body that explode in colors of pain and I silently beg to return to the numbness I left behind, from dreams I escape to, and sometimes I am carried to, but always return from, these dreams in which I search for someone named Lucas but never find him, and in these moments between sleep's twilight and awakening I welcome death, wish it even, but it never comes and I am ashamed of the tears that pool in the corners of my eyes, unable to brush them away with my hands still chained to weighted arms, impossible to move, eyes that see nothing and know everything and the impossible wave of grief that crushes me in the awakening and convinces me there are worse things than death.

And when the beasts are with me, tearing me apart, I see his blue eyes beckoning me forward, come away, be free, and I try to reach out my hand to take his, but I am shackled to this hell and cannot. I hear the roar of the ocean, but realize it is my own voice, screaming.

Who am I?

14.

The children found him late in the afternoon trussed to a cottonwood tree with the high heat of the afternoon's sun bearing down on him, his hands bound behind, his legs spread-eagled in the dirt. They had seen the vultures circling above, harbingers that practiced patience like a termite eats wood—diligently, with a great deal of persistence, understanding time is on their side.

Ruby stood several yards off in the scrub and looked up briefly when the children arrived. They formed a half circle around JT and watched him struggle to free his hands, twisting against the rope violently, only succeeding in burning the jute into his wrists, the skin now raw. Flies rested on the sweat trickled in the cleft of his throat. He shook his head to rid them, but they immediately returned. The vision in his right eye blurred.

"Ayuda," JT said. But the children remained impassive and stared. Some looked to an older girl in the group.

"Ayuda. Por favor."

The older girl stepped forward. Her hand gripped a small brown paper bag. She knelt and opened the sack, shaking its contents onto the desert floor, a few feet from JT's boots. From the bag a tarantula dropped, the size of his fist.

"Damn," JT said.

Not many things spooked JT like spiders did. He had history with the arachnids, none of it good. When he was four, an Apache brown jumped clear across the barn rafters and bit him, causing a fever that spiraled to 104 and up. Ma said she held a vigil for two days praying him alive. A few years after that he disturbed a black widow's den on a rock ledge while jumping into the creek. The sting caused muscle spasms that nearly drowned him before Harlan dragged him out. But the worst was when Pa punished him for busting the shaving fork when mucking out the stables and locked him in the shed overnight, a windowless shack whose dirt floor stunk of mold and dead things. A nest of wolf spiders occupied the corners, their bodies as large as half-dollars and their long-haired legs steepled beneath them, eyes like black pebbles aglow in the dark. He spent hours in complete blackness, every cell of his body awake, jerking when he felt the breeze of something creep across his skin, begging to be let him out until Harlan jangled the keys and unlocked the door, finding him bathed in sweat. Two days later he and his brother lit a rag doused in kerosene and burned the shed to the ground, along with every spider in it. Ever since JT avoided them at all costs. The terror he felt for wolf spiders paled in comparison to the tarantula headed towards him now.

"Ayuda, niños, por favor." His voice strained.

Another child stepped forward. She held a stick up for JT to see, then jabbed it at the spider, sending it scrabbling towards JT's feet.

"Shit." JT pulled his feet up under him, keeping his eye fixed on the bug coming towards him. Seeing his fright, the children squealed in delight.

"Bailas," they said, and one pirouetted. A boy took the stick from the girl and poked the tarantula again, making it hiss.

"Basta," JT said. The more his feet tried to gain traction, the more dust he kicked up, and the sillier he looked. The children screamed in delight, clapping their hands together. The tarantula tried to retreat, but the children used the sticks to keep moving it forward.

"Bailas," they said again.

JT whistled for Ruby and the children parted as the horse came forward. But when she approached the tarantula, she stepped back, pawing the ground and shaking her head, neighing. The spider stopped and sat motionless.

"C'mon girl." JT whistled again and Ruby moved closer, lowering her head to the ground, blowing air from her nostrils. The tarantula darted, and the horse shied. The spider jumped onto JT's right boot, and the children could not contain their laughter.

"I'm not fooling now." The rigor in his voice took on threads of fear. A woolly, striped leg reached out to touch the firmness of the boot and then scrambled up across the calf leather. JT shook his leg but it had a firm grip. The children giggled and moved closer. JT pushed his body back against the tree, trying to raise himself to a standing position and as he did, his hat slid against the trunk, falling from his head.

"Mira," one of the children said. They stopped laughing and stared at JT. The skin on the right side of his brow glowed reddish-pink while the inner edges of the gash were swollen and white. Dried blood, now black, filled the opening. The children forgot the spider, their eyes focused on the bulging infection spreading across JT's brow.

"Andale!" A man's voice came from behind the tree. "Andale!" He clapped his hands in the air. The startled children yowled and fled, dropping their sticks and scattering. The man picked up a discarded stick and leveraged it beneath the tarantula squatting on JT's thigh. Deftly he flipped the spider into the air, sending it spiraling into the scrub. The tightness in JT's chest loosened. He felt a tug on the rope binding his hands, and then he was free.

"Muchas gracias," JT said. He rubbed his chaffed wrists, then turned toward his redeemer. He was Mexican, in his late forties perhaps, and crippled. He sat atop a planked board, one side sawed off, the other side splintered, its underside connected to a large wheel. The man's legs lay twisted underneath him in an unnatural pose and years of balancing his weight kept the board below him horizontal. A half-smoked cigarette hung from his mouth. He studied JT, taking a deep drag on the cigarette and letting the smoke curl out between his lips. His eyes drifted to JT's forehead. JT put his fingers to the wound then pulled them back as the touch sent stabs of pain through the swollen skin. He picked up his hat and with it the bandana, the cloth slimy and wet. He eased the hat back onto his head, keeping the bandana between the skin and the hat's band. The Mexican watched him do this and said nothing.

"Gracias de nuevo," JT said.

"Donde esta su amigo?"

JT looked in the direction he last saw Roy with the soldiers. "Con el Federales."

The man coughed, then spat on the ground. "Quien?"

"El Federales."

"No hay Federales."

"Tenían uniformes."

For a moment the man's face was blank, then he laughed and repeated what he had said, that there were no Federales.

"Entonces, quién?"

The man shrugged and continued to smoke. JT took a step and a wave of dizziness overtook him. He placed his hand on the tree to steady himself. The man watched.

"¿A dónde vas?" the man asked.

"Juárez."

The man nodded.

"¿Hasta dónde?" JT said.

"¿A Juárez?"

"Sí."

The man thought on this a while. "¿Éste su caballo?"

"Sí."

The Mexican studied the horse. "Quatro noches a Juárez." he said, holding up four fingers of his right hand.

JT asked the man how long it would take if he travelled day as well as night.

The man looked at Ruby again, then at JT. He flicked the butt of his cigarette into the bush and using his hands pushed his cart onto the road. "Viajar día y noche está invitando a los buitres," he said, pointing to the birds above, "a cenar."

JT looked up at the vultures circling in the sky. When he turned back, the man was gone.

The mountains of the Chihuahuan Desert wavered in the heat, the air heavy with the smell of creosote as he and Ruby moved along its carpeted curves, across the wind-swept expense of sand where secreted life pulsated. They walked quail up out of the scrub and came across herds of grazing white tail deer who seemed curious of their presence, their heads lifting as JT walked the horse down the mesa corridors, trap rock falling away beneath the horse's feet. The shadow of a zone-tailed hawk swept along the canyon wall until it came fully into view, the wind suspending its wings on pockets of air, its call a high-pitched scream. Down the slope of the mountain they passed stands of shindagger, sprouting their long stalks from rock ledges, spiny-toothed edges bladed against predators and the desert heat. JT paused, reaching for his canteen and sat the horse while he drank and surveyed his surroundings.

The sand he crossed was forgiving of tracks, the bullying wind erasing any trace of the path the uniformed men traveled. Each time he entertained thoughts of finding Roy, thoughts of Dalia pulled him in the opposite direction, towards Juárez. As the sun lowed itself behind the mountains, then below the horizon's lip, the sky turning a brilliant explosion of orange-red, all he could think about was time and needing more of it and having no idea where it could be purchased. And the cost. He cursed the cost.

By the time the moon stood above him, unabashed and scolding in the Saharan-like silence, his hopes of finding Roy were exhausted. A shivering wracked his body. He told himself it was the cooling of the desert, the absence of day's heat, but he knew it was more than that. He fed the horse from the sack of oats, pouring it into his hat and holding it while she ate, then staked her near a shallow tinaja where she lapped at the water. Camped in the lee of a small volcano, its bulk solid against the black night, he fell into a fitful sleep that roused him twice awake, only to realize the stars still occupied the sky. In the early morning he woke to the drumming of drizzling rain, his head throbbing, so thickly weighted he could barely lift it from the head of his bedroll. His clothes were soaked in chilled dampness and a small shudder convulsed him. He rose, feeling 100 pounds heavier, a gauzy fog inside his head. He saddled Ruby and rode on.

Traveling east, the landscape shifted, leaving him with miles of low white-powdered hills scattered with greasewood and tarbush, the sand dusting Ruby's legs while the sun hammered down. Each stretch looked the same as the last one, and soon he feared he was caught in a loop retracing the same steps again and again, trapped in a labyrinth of blistered sand. If Harlan's voice hadn't spoken to him, telling him to lift his eyes and turn back, he would have missed the tracks altogether. *Dammit, JT, get your head out of the toilet. You can't afford stupid mistakes like this.* He knew it too. A cold sweat broke across his brow and he wiped it with the sleeve of his shirt.

He reined the horse to a stop and swung down from the saddle, the heels of his boots barely making a mark in the dryness of the desert's dirt. He stared at the tracks, then knelt down and ran his fingers lightly over the grooves where each horse's hoof weighted its mark in the sand, dipping his finger into the rutted imprints to gauge their depression. Five horses in all, each carrying a rider. He squinted, looking at the direction they came from and then the trail south, where they led, realizing that more than a score of riders could have passed through this wilderness in the past two weeks. The hope he secreted lay blandly stretched, unwilling to voice its opinion. And while he knelt there in sundered indecision, hoping for Harlan's voice to speak to him again, his eye caught sight of a gleaming in the distance. When he stood, it disappeared from sight, so he stooped again, realizing the exact angle at which he knelt made it possible to see the shimmer. He stayed that way, crawling on his hands and knees towards the glint he imagined was abalone shell, pausing when he thought he lost it and moving quickly forward when he saw it again. Anyone watching would think he'd gone mad, scrambling wildly on his knees across the desert floor, his horse trailing behind him. Finally he reached the spot and with his hands sifted through the earth until he felt the thing touch his fingers. He grabbed at it, holding it up, shielding his eyes from the sand that fell away. It was a horseshoe, worn and dusted in the desert heat. He stared at it, trying to remember where he was, and what in god's name had brought him to his knees. A ragged breath escaped his lips, his hand trembling as he closed his fist around the metal shoe, then flung it far beyond the wizened landscape. He leaned back on his knees and remained that way for a breath and wept.

As he made to stand, a massive throbbing racked his head and both eyes blurred. He reached out to take a hold of the saddle and missed, laying hold of the horse's mane. Like a blind man he felt along the horse, grabbed hold of the horn, and hoisted himself into the saddle. His effort was rewarded with another chill that chased his backbone. A fever was drawing down upon him, a shivered rush of gooseflesh warning him he needed to find shelter. Soon.

He pushed Ruby forward, over the scrabbled tracks, and down into the arroyo in the westerly direction of Juárez. An hour passed and with his vision almost completely blurred, he spied what he thought were drafts of smoke a mile or so off to the northwest. He turned the horse in that direction. Twenty minutes later he came to a mud-thatched adobe dwelling, the windows and door made from weathered flaps of animal skin.

"Hola," he called out. Then waited. A woman appeared at the flapped door, only her face showing, her gaze stoic.

"Hola, Señora."

The woman said nothing. Her expression remained blank.

"Por favor. Estoy enfermo."

Her expression remained blank, watching him with hawked eyes. "Hmf," she said, then disappeared behind the animal skin. He waited but she did not return. When he could wait no longer he swung down. Shudders raced his spine and his temples fevered in waves of heat.

Again he tried to remember why he was here. Then suddenly the ground rose up to meet him and he was on his knees, imagining himself praying. The very last thing he clearly remembered was falling forward, into a fire.

15.

H e woke in slivered darkness, a burning thirst so insatiable that everything except water was driven from his thoughts. He tried to swallow, the dryness of his throat catching. The air smelled of simmered cocoa and fried oil. A hand reached behind his head, bringing him forward, then water was at his lips. He sucked at it, not knowing what shape of container it lay in, nor the amount, nor when it would disappear.

"Despacio." The voice assured him there was more water to be had.

"Gracias." His voice was slow, hoarse. "How many days?

"¿Qué?"

"Cuántos dias?"

"Dos."

Two days. Two days I've let her down. Two days I'll never get back.

A wet cloth fell across his forehead, coarse burlap that smelled of raw beans.

"Gracias."

Above him a black-eyed Mexican girl swam, her skin the color of baked clay. "Duérmete," she said.

"No."

"Sí. Duérmete."

She tilted her head while he tried to lift his hands in protest but could not. The rumble of distant thunder reached his ears and with it the dryness in his throat returned.

"Tu nombre?" he said, his voice now whispered, the exercise to speak an effort.

She smiled. Behind her soft light stirred, framing her head. The glow hurt his eyes and he closed them. When he opened them again she was gone.

J T *blew out the match and stood up. He knew better than to strike flame in the thick of an August wheat crop but couldn't bring to mind why. The yellowed durum stalks sagged towards him, hugging his body as he shifted his weight amongst them, the rolled cigarette threaded to his lips with spit. Thunder growled but blue skies refused to yield and he walked on. Sweat beaded at his hairline and crackling sighs made him turn behind to face the fields of wheat yawed out in flames. The cigarette gone from his mouth.*

He started awake, thirsty and bathed in sweat. Blood drummed his ears and he waited out its retreat while his breathing slowed. Light filled the room spilling from square holes in the wall dug out from the adobe brick. A wooden spike stabbed into the mud beside each hole swept back an animal hide resting in the wood's crook. He stared at the tawny sorrel pattern on the hide and for a moment he imagined it was the cur, skinned and drawn-out before him then his eyes widened, and he saw it was not. Hung between the windows, a wooden *crucifijo* lay nailed to the wall, dried palm leaves curled around it, brittle and dusty.

The dwelling was partitioned into three rooms: the room in which he lay, a middle room, and a room opposite with a closed door. Outlines of furniture, their exactness beyond his seeing, shadowed the middle room. Looking upward, each eye movement slow and deliberate, paper dolled cutouts scissored from a child's hand dangled below the ceiling in the middle room. A small breeze caught hold of them and they danced, tugging each other forward then back. Human shapes moved against the backdrop of the adjoining room where voices fell and rose. The deep chords of another voice intertwined the voices, and JT struggled to lift himself up but could not.

"Hola?" he said, lifting his arm with effort. It wavered in the air then fell. The señora whose face he first saw outside the dwelling appeared above him.

"Agua. Por favor."

The woman held the back of his neck and tipped a cup to his lips. Tepid water that tasted of iron settled his thirst.

"Gracias."

The wet burlap was placed across his brow and water trickled into his hair. When it came away, he could see traces of black blood along its length. Pain traveled his forehead. She dipped the cloth in water and squeezed the wetness from it, replacing it on his skin. Her eyes resisted meeting his and he remained quiet while she spoke and told him he arrived two days ago with a bad fever that nearly took his life. An infection had swelled deep in the gash on his forehead and had to be cleaned. She told him it was fortunate for him that the fever rendered him unconscious because the pain would have been too great to bear.

"Muy doloroso," she said.

He watched her through narrowed eyes, the vision in his right completely blurred. Her arms were brown sticks that moved and crossed above him, her unsmiling face drawn serious between black hair bound loosely behind her neck, strands brushed with gray at their roots. Her skin hinted at sweat and smelled like clay and the color red, something he faintly recognized but could not place. And when she laid the burlap against his forehead, he felt the strength of her hands, the hands of a thousand tasks, a thousand burdens, in the space of one lifetime, from the time she unlearned to smile.

"¿Mi caballo?"

"Está bien."

The woman said that he and his horse must leave as soon as the illness passed. JT tried to raise himself up on his elbows but faltered and fell back. The woman told him it was not yet time, that he was not well enough to leave the house. He must wait until he was well or they would find him some miles from here in the arroyo, dead, his eyes pecked blind. He would be easy to find, following the buzzards readying themselves for the feast. She would not have this bad omen on her house and on her family. They had suffered enough.

"Demasiado," she said, shaking her head.

"¿De qué manera?"

But she refused to speak of the ways in which they had suffered and removed the cloth from his forehead and moved away with the bowl and the cloth. She came back several minutes later and pulled the straw from underneath the wooden pallet on which he lay. It smelled of urine and must, and she carried it outside the house. She returned with fresh straw that smelled of pig and laid it underneath the bed.

"¿Tienes hambre?" she said.

"No."

"Necesitas comer." She was gone and soon he heard the shuffling of pans and plates. The young girl, mute and fisheyed came into view above him.

"¿Cuál es tu nombre?" he asked, in a soft voice.

"Lupita."

"Lupita," he repeated.

In the kitchen, bowls clattered to the floor.

"¡Mantenerse lejos de él!"

He turned in the direction of the senora's voice. When he turned back the girl was gone.

The next day he awoke and lifted himself up on his elbows. His fever had subsided and with it the throbbing in his head. The rank smell of manure came from outside where he heard the lazy bray of a donkey. Two chickens scuttled into the house in a flurry of feathers and pecked their way across the mud floor. He looked down at the serape covering his body, stained with streaks of rust greased lines, and at the end of the wool he saw his feet, white and bare and feeling wholly detached from the rest of him. He stared at them as if they were foreign and belonged to another being altogether. When he raised his eyes a man stood alongside the cot. He introduced himself as the woman's husband. JT struggled to push himself into a sitting position, leaning his back against the wall at the head of the cot. The man watched without offering to help. He asked JT what business had brought him to Mexico.

"Busco a alguien," JT said.

"¿Dónde?"

"Juárez."

"¿Una mujer?"

JT said yes, he was looking for a girl and how did the man know this. The man shrugged. He said that in his experience, there are few men who would travel into the belly of the serpent for reasons other than love.

"¿Porque?"

The man said that love is a thing that cannot be ignored, but once set in motion is difficult to reason with. It follows no rules. Those who think they can change this are wrong because it is the other way around. It changes them. He said that this was a simple truth, but one that no man wants to hear.

"¿Crees esto?" the man said.

"No sé."

"¿Has estado en Juárez?"

JT shook his head and said he had never been.

The man studied the boy, as if deciding whether to tell him a great secret and that choosing the right words were of utmost importance. Finally he spoke. He said that Juárez was a godless place where dreams die and misfortunates live in the company of violence. The streets boasted malice and greed, and creatures not recognizable to the human eye. Love did not exist in such a place and were the boy to search for it there, he would not find it. Or at the very least, what he found would not be what he lost.

The man called to his wife and his wife came from the kitchen and brought him a cup of water which he offered to JT.

"Gracias." JT took the cup in both hands and drank. "Ella está ahí. Estoy seguro."

The man thought on this. Then he said that a man who trusts his heart is a man to be pitied.

"¿Por qué?"

"Porque de valientes y apasionado están llenos los panteones." *Because cemeteries are full of the courageous and impassioned*, words he recited as though practicing all his life.

JT ran his fingers over the cut on his forehead. "A veces hay que creer en lo que sientes."

The man shrugged. "Tal vez," he said, but in his experience the man who trusts his heart risks being undone. The pity is they do not understand that what they seek is not the piety of love, but the hypocrisy of lust. A familiar mistake. Dangerous too. The blind man must remember who sits to his right and who sits to his left so that he does not look the fool.

"¿Y tú? ¿Cometes este error?" the man asked.

"No."

"¿Cómo puede estar seguro?

"Lo sé."

JT and the man sat in silence. Then the man spoke. "Por supuesto que sí."

The man said JT should get some sleep, and that they would talk again tomorrow. JT said that he would be well enough to leave tomorrow and at this the man laughed. It did not matter whether he thinks he is well or not. His wife is very superstitious and would not let him leave until she thought he was well. JT should save his strength. He would need it where he was going.

That night JT woke to the sound of raised voices coming from behind the closed door. The man and the woman argued. He lifted himself up on his elbows where he could see Lupita sitting in the corner of the middle room, her legs crossed, rocking. A low keening accompanied the rocking and her eyes remained fixed on the door. JT whispered to her but she would not acknowledge him. He lay back down and listened to the sounds until sleep overtook him again.

In his dreams it was the cur that keened as it stood in front of him, hackles raised, face twisted into a snarl. It bared its white-yellow teeth and came forward, out of the fire, its fur singed, and he climbed onto its back and they flew from the earth out into the sky.

The next day the man brought with him a chair from the table in the outer room and placed it at the side of the pallet. He sat and lit a cigarette, then blew out a thin line of smoke that lifted into the air and disappeared.

"Cigarette?"

"No. Gracias."

They sat in silence while the man smoked.

The man said he would like to tell him a story. He said this was the first time he told this story out loud but that his wife insisted it be told and he listens to his wife in matters such as these because she has the gift of seeing. The man took a deep drag on his cigarette and continued. He said that all stories do not have happy endings, so JT should not look for one, and warned that if he was to be interrupted, he may not be able to finish. He took another deep drag and began.

The man said that your children hold the secrets of everything you wished to be, the things out of your reach. You see through them the beauty of the world again, as if for the first time. They fall short of your expectations, sometimes, because you are too busy shaping their lives to see that they are on the path of their own expectations which are very different than yours and should be because they are, themselves, unique—not repeats of the parent. "Nos olvidamos de eso." *We forget that.* Never do you let yourself imagine for one moment that they will die and cease to exist, and soon you begin to believe this as truth. The act of a father who buries his child is a wronging, a blasphemy of nature, and with this act is buried the promise of all things good in the world and things that should come to pass and the covenant to protect the ones needing protection, the covenant we make with God and ourselves and those we love.

He raised the cigarette to his lips and inhaled, then released his breath and continued.

Sometimes there is a middle place, somewhere between the living and dying. It is a place where the child exists, but still the child is lost to you. In the beginning you give great thanks that He has spared you their death. Spared you the pain of never seeing your child again. But as time passes, you come to realize this is not a gift. This is simply a different kind of death.

Until finally you recognize nothing of the child you once loved. "Es un ... ¿cómo se dice .... paradoja?

"Sí. A paradox."

The cigarette's ash had grown long and as the man lifted the tobacco to his mouth, the powder fell to his feet.

"Sí," the man continued. A mystery, this middle place between death and life. It pays tribute to false hope. No healing takes place, you see, because it stares you in the face until it contaminates all you touch. Everything. You have the child, but you have lost the child. It is as you say, a paradoja. And in the end you have failed both the child and your ability to heal. The cigarette hung suspended in the air in front of his lips, as though he had forgotten its purpose. Then he moved it away from his lips. "Más remedio tiene un muerto." *Even a dead man has more to hope for.*

JT followed the man's gaze. Lupita sat cross-legged on the floor, facing the holes in the mud. She sat unmoving, her eyes blank. In one hand folded paper, in the other scissors. But she did not put the one to the other. Her mouth formed words with no sound and she grimaced, then grinned.

"Es tu hija?" JT said.

"Sí."

"Es ella de quien hablas?"

The man raised a trembling hand to his mouth and drew on the cigarette. As he exhaled the smoke snaked from his nose.

"Sí," he said, his voice old.

JT waited for him to speak again, but he did not. The man dropped the cigarette on the dirt floor. Then he rose from the chair and left.

16.

At night JT awoke to the sound of raised voices beyond the closed door, and the keening in the outer room that accompanied it, but the man never returned.

In the morning he experienced a gnawing in his stomach and was surprised to recognize he was hungry. He swung his feet over the side of the pallet, touching the hard clay of the dirt floor. The fogged numbness in his head was gone and he could now see clearly out of his right eye. His fingers touched the uneven spate of stitches above his brow. The pain was gone, the scar tentative.

The woman appeared soon after he woke, bringing with her a tray of watery eggs and tortillas and a small cloth. He accepted the tray onto his lap and waited, the smell of food consuming him, making the ache in his stomach tighten.

"Comer."

He nodded and turned his attention to the eggs and ate, sopping them up with the tortillas.

"Bien," she said. It was a good sign. She pulled a chair to the side of his pallet and in silence she watched him eat. JT wiped his mouth with the cloth and took a drink from the cup of water she offered. After he swallowed the last bites, she spoke.

"¿Qué te ha dicho?"

He told the woman all that her husband had said, and when he finished the woman's eyes were wet and she stared at her hands, loosely folded in her lap.

"¿Nada más?"

"No."

The woman said that she would tell him what her husband could not.

"Por favor."

She said their daughter, Lupita, was stolen from them when she was 13 years of age.

"¿Por quién?"

The woman shook her head. By the traffickers, devils who run the whorehouses in Juárez. Hyenas who single out the weak and vulnerable then wait for an opportunity to present itself. It happens every day in her country and it seems they are without means to stop it.

"¿Qué pasó?"

The woman looked towards the girl in the middle room. Her husband and son Miguel travelled to Juárez and were gone for many days, but by God's grace they found Lupita and brought her back. How they did this, she had no idea. The woman stopped and touched her right eye with the hem of her shirt. She said she could not talk of the unspeakable things done to her daughter, in part because she does not know. It is something her husband will not speak about and she cannot bring herself to ask.

She paused and leaned her elbows on her knees, resting her mouth against her clasped hands. Then she drew a deep breath and continued. She said that Lupita was not the only one harmed. That a price was paid by both her husband and her son, witnessing their daughter, his sister, lying in filth, men upon her. A price that would never again allow them to look at her daughter, or the world, in the same way as before. She explained that it is like having a loved one cut into pieces and you are called to identify the body. This is the last memory you have of this person, so this is the one that stays in your head and replays. It is what you see when you think of them, how you remember them, even though you do not want to. She paused, turning her head, then quietly repeated, "No deseas."

"¿Dónde está tu hijo?

"Miguel está muerto."

"¿Muerto?"

She said that Miguel went to rescue his sister but did not return from Juárez.

"Pero usted dijo—"

"Su hermana menor."

"¿Una hija más joven?" He was surprised to learn Lupita had a younger sister.

"Sí. Graciela."

"¿Y cuántos años—?"

"Once."

"Eleven?

"Sí."

"*Eleven.*" JT turned the number over in his head. He looked blankly past the woman, his eyes searching but not seeing, until they came to rest on the crucifix on the wall. He stared at it, following the shadowed lines of the Christ figure stretched taut on the wood, his dhoti stained red, nails jutting from his hands and feet. The woman followed his gaze.

"¿Hombres nacen de esta manera?"

"¿Señora?"

She repeated her words, asking him if he thought men were born this way, with evil in their hearts. She said she would like to believe not. She would like to believe that when they issue from their mother's womb, the souls of men still carry the grace from the world they left, before their feet touch earth. That no man is born wicked for purposes of sin. She spoke these words while she too gazed at the crucifix. "No," she continued, she could not believe men were born this way because the God she knows does not create wickedness, children robbed of their souls. She asked JT if he believed this.

"That this is not the same God?"

She shook her head and asked if he believed men were born this way.

He stared at the crucifix again, then looked to the room where Lupita sat, mouthing words with no sound. Then he told the woman that he hoped she was right—that men created by God were not born this way. But he added that he had known men in his lifetime who made him think otherwise.

"¿Dónde está Graciela ahora?"

"No sé." No, that was not true. Graciela was in Juárez, but where in Juárez they did not know. Miguel never returned to tell them.

A soft breeze stirred the animal hide on the square holes in the wall and for a brief moment cloud cover draped the dwelling, darkening the rooms. Then it was gone and light filtered into the room.

"How will I know her?"

"¿Qué?"

"Is this not why you told me the story? To find Graciela in Juarez?"

"Quiero mi esposo haga esto."

Her words puzzled JT. Did her husband not want to find his youngest child?

The woman looked away. She said that this was a question she has asked of her husband many times. She is not certain even he knows the answer.

JT thought about the man and their conversation. *A different kind of death. Una paradoja.*

"How will I know her? Tienes una foto?"

"No," the woman said. But when Graciela was eight years old, she was kicked by a mule and the hoof left a scar that runs from the top of her left eyebrow down the length of the left side of her face close to her ear. The woman used her hand to trace the position of the scar on her own face, then did so again on JT's face. It was not a deep scar, but one that would be visible to those who knew where to look.

"No te puedo prometer," JT said.

"Comprendo." She said she hated to ask this of him but knew of no one else to turn to. Every day she has prayed for a miracle, and she was on her knees in front of the Madonna when JT appeared at her door four days ago. When she learned of his plans to travel to Juárez, she believed her prayers had been answered.

Lupita's cries came from the other room. She held the scissors in one hand, the other hand was lifted into the air. Her mother crossed the room and knelt down to examine the wounded finger. "Está bien," she said, folding her daughter into her arms, rocking her while they sat on the dirt floor.

Early the next morning JT rose and dressed in the cambered light filtering through the square holes in the adobe walls. His clothes were folded at the foot of his cot, clean and dried, the crusted blood in his bandana gone. The band of his hat had been scrubbed, the slickness removed, yet still a dark stain remained.

In the lean-to he talked to Ruby while he saddled her, tightening the latigo and leaving the cinch loose. He checked the hooves for bruising, then mounted and walked her outside. In front of the adobe dwelling he stopped and lifted his hat to the woman and her daughter standing in the doorway. The woman handed him food done up in a cloth which he took and put in the saddlebag underneath his jacket. She shielded her eyes with her right hand and looked up at his form, silhouetted black against the sun. He nodded, touching a thumb to the brim of his hat, then put the horse forward. As he reached the corner of the house, her husband appeared and came forward atop the mule. For a brief moment they studied each other, then together moved off across the desert at a slow trot. When they reached the crest of the first ridge, both men looked back towards the adobe dwelling. The woman still stood in the doorway, holding her hand to her eyes.

JT asked the man if the woman knew he would go.

"¿Cómo podría?" The man asked how she could know when he, himself, did not know until that very minute.

17.

They travelled east across the northern meseta of the Chihuahuan Desert, then south across Highway 2, where they could see the blinding white of los Medanos de Samalayuca, billowed sand heaped like canopied tents lofted with poles of varying length. They rode without speaking across the spattering of greasewood and tarbrush huddled in monotypic stands on the dry barren flatland. A brace of mule deer stood off in the distance and lifted their heads at the broken silence caused by the plodding horses. A gray fox darted from underneath a catclaw shrub, then disappeared across the desert. Soft whistled murmurs of wind shifted in a constant state of flux, dipping in and out of curves reshaped into the landscape. To the east, Cuidad Juárez spread out on the floor below in a carpet of geometrical design like veins in a human body, simmering in the heat of the noonday sun. At the base of the dunes they stopped, resting the horses and ate the food the woman had packed.

The man asked JT how he knew the girl he looked for was still alive.

"I don't," JT said.

The man nodded and ate. When they finished he rolled a cigarette and lit the end with a match struck against the side of the rock. "Dígame sobre esta chica."

"Her name is—"

"No. I no care for names. ¿Qué cómo se ve?"

He hesitated in describing her, worried about his choice of words, as if not picking the right ones would bring harm, put her at risk somehow, much like a secret incantation that you must get right the first utterance upon peril of sudden death. Once he started, it surprised him how much detail he remembered, the musked green of her eyes glinted with amber, the slow curve of her chin, smooth and strong. When he came to mention the color of her hair, the man held up his hand.

"No mas," he said. He took a drag on his cigarette and said he was certain the girl was still alive.

"Cómo sabes?"

"Esta especial."

"Sí."

"No," the man said. "Especial in Juárez."

The man studied the boy to see if he understood and saw by the hardening in JT's jaw that he did. He told him that this could be a good thing or bad thing.

"¿Qué tan bueno?"

The man told him that it would be a hard thing to destroy a rare jewel. An unlikely thing. And that if she is in Juárez, she would not be so easy to hide.

"¿Qué tan mal?"

The man shrugged and drew on the tobacco again, exhaling the smoke into the wind. He said that the rarer the jewel, the more coveted it is, the higher price it would bring.

"You're saying that they might have sold her."

"¿Qué?

"Vendido. La vendió.

The man didn't answer right away. Then he said, yes, this was true.

The food in JT's mouth had no taste. He turned his head and spat, then ran the sleeve of his shirt across his mouth.

"Separamos aquí," the man said. He could not guarantee they would not recognize him from before.

148

Wolves take notice of who is in their barrios. He knelt down and with his left hand smoothed the sand flat and used the remainder of his cigarette to draw intersecting lines depicting the streets and avenues of the Mariscal district. He explained that this was where the whorehouses could be found. He told JT that he would see things in Juárez that would be foreign to him, that he would not understand, and counseled him to ignore them. They would distract him. Be certain to stay clear of *los descuenteros*, men who lure unsuspecting ones into alleys and side streets with promises, then cut and rob them. They would meet again in this same place after they found who they came for. Then he mounted the mule.

"Uno cosa más, hijo," the man said as he reined the mule in JT's direction. He told him to be prepared that the girl he searched for will not be the same as before. That she will be changed in a way he will not wish to see. He understood this, yes? Tell him now.

JT looked down at his boots. He felt the sun's heat on the back of his neck. Then he looked back at the man.

"Sí. Comprendo."

The man nodded, then put his heels to the mule and rode off. In a matter of moments he was a small figure obscured by dust in the animal's wake. A strong wind blew up around JT, making him take hold of his hat. Sand dusted his eyes. He prayed the man was wrong.

B y mid-afternoon the streets of Juárez were beginning to crowd, vendors panhandling blankets, serapes, cheap jewelry and food. The scent of roasted chilies thickened the air together with the fermented odor of urine and beer. JT entered the city from the southwest end and made his way to the Mariscal district. Young boys ran after him with empty tin cans, hands outstretched begging money—almost demanding. He paid one of the boys a dollar to hold Ruby in check and promised another dollar when he returned. An American couple passed him in the street, their arms draped around each other, full of drink, walking towards the Paso del Norte Bridge. There was no sign of Lupita's father.

Small establishments lined Juárez Avenue, their outside walls in faded pastels, dulled by the sun, peeling paint covering splintered plywood. He entered a blue house through a green door and sat at the bar. The room was smoky and dark, and JT waited until his eyes adjusted to the shadows. The first thing he saw was a well-dressed Mexican behind the bar watching him over the rim of the glass he was drying. He ordered a beer. The bartender went away and came back with a draft that he placed in front of JT. Another customer signaled a refill and the man moved down the bar, retrieving the whiskey and filling the glass. His eyes kept watch in JT's direction.

A dark-skinned girl, no more than twelve or thirteen years of age approached JT, the red rouge of her cheeks matching her lipstick.

"You like?" she said, in English, pirouetting in a small circle before him.

"Muy bonita," JT said.

The girl took his hand and tried to draw him from the bar stool.

"No. No gracias." JT said.

"Come on, Señor Cowboy," she said pulling his sleeve.

"No." he said gently pulling his arm away.

The girl gave a small scowl and moved to the next customer at the neighboring stool whose widening smile promised a better fare. JT turned to look at the rest of the whores lounging on the worn sofas and chairs, attached to other men in the bar. They were young, but it was hard to gauge how young with the pancaked makeup and overarched eyeliner. None of them were Dalia. He watched each girl as she turned her head, and he saw no scar running the length of the left side of their face.

"¿Qué quieres?" the bartender asked.

"¿Qué?"

"What is it you want?"

"A drink. Es todo." JT downed the beer and placed the empty glass on the counter.

"You have had your drink. Vamos," the bartender said.

"Una más, por favor."

The bartender leaned both hands, spread apart, on the shined cherry wood of the bar top and stared at JT. "I don't like you," he said. Then he tapped the table with the flat of his palm, twice. From a dark corner of the bar a large Mexican man stepped from the shadows.

JT rose from his stool and picked up his hat from the tabletop. "No problema. Gracias."

Outside he winced as the sun hit his eyes. A strong wind blew across, carrying with it clouds of dust and dirt, little pieces of discarded wrappers littering the street, cigarette stubs and the faint smell of ammonia rising from the trash in the alley next to the building. He stepped into another establishment on the same street a few houses down that reeked of the same seediness he had just come from. He ordered a beer and watched the girls. An hour passed before he left the bar and entered yet another one. A half hour later he stepped out into the street once more, the light fading to afternoon dusk. He scanned the street trying to decide which of the brothels would yield more clues than the rest, but nothing in their appearance suggested he was closer to finding her than before. He walked down Ignacio Melia Street to Santos Delgados. There stood another surplus of squalid row houses. Ranchera music increased and drifted away as doors opened and closed. It suddenly occurred to him that finding Dalia in this labyrinth of aduanas was almost beyond the bounds of possibility. A weariness came over him and a profound sadness he hadn't felt since Harlan died.

Turn, a voice inside his head said. And so he did.

Behind him sprawled a trail of street vendors, their urgent voices raised in fervor at the passersby. They guaranteed satisfaction on all purchases, their pockets bulged with wads of rolled bills they peeled off when making change. JT stared hard, waiting for the voice inside his head to continue, but nothing. A group of teenagers with hollowed out guitars played mariachi music while two young girls danced in the street, and the streets milled with throngs of people, buying, selling, trading. He stood transfixed, hope dwindling, combing the crowd for a sign, any sign. Then he saw it.

A black-haired girl stood in the company of customers and in her hair the color of silver. The way the sun dropped low caused the glint resting on the hairpin. Crested at the top of her crown, neatly pinned, was the hairpin Dalia wore the last time he saw her. The sheen of the abalone shell had caught the last rays of the sun, the iridescent mother-of-pearl shimmering like a mirage in the desert. JT moved toward it as if in a trance, all sound drowned out by the quickening of his pulse. A small child darted in front of him, upsetting a cart and the merchant howled at the child, throwing up his hands in annoyance. The woman turned sharply at the commotion and JT stopped. He had been so mesmerized by the hairpin that he failed to realize the girl in no way resembled Dalia. And yet, he was certain the pin was hers. The woman glanced at him briefly then went back to her task at hand. She pointed to a chicken which the vendor retrieved, then stepped on his neck and slit its throat, letting the blood spill out onto the pavement until the pulsating stopped. He wrapped it in newspaper and handed it to the woman, accepting the pesos she deposited in his hand. Then she moved on.

He followed her at a distance. Hawkers called to him from their perches, their voices swallowed up in the melee. The hairpin vanished into the crowd and a panic seized him before catching sight of the woman re-emerge at the end of the street. Two blocks further she entered an alley and disappeared into a red door. He walked to the front of the building where the name *Blue Swan*, was painted on a sign above the front door. A Mexican emerged from the building and he grabbed hold of the door before it closed and went in.

The darkness of the room was tempered with lamps that sat on end tables flanking the sides of a worn Chesterfield sofa. The dimness hid the worn spots on the red velour upholstery and the aged cigarette burns. The sofa was crowded with girls and paying customers, some laying on top of each other, one man licking the spilled alcohol from a woman's breast. The wall above the sofa was paneled with square smoked glass mirrors stained with gold colored brocade, cheap imitations of an antique look. They picked up the light from across the room facing it where another panel of mirrors ran the length behind the bar. The floor was carpeted in dark green that hid the dirt's grime and trapped the drowned smoke passed around the room.

Laughter filled the opposite end of the bar where a group of regulars sat, their glasses full to empty, loud and raucous. He sat on a stool and ordered a beer, then watched the whores in the bar's mirror work the room behind him while he waited. The bottle was half way to his lips when he heard the ratchet of a gun's hammer pulled back against his ear.

"Mira quien tenemos aquí."

JT lowered his beer to the bar and turned. The Mexican holding the gun to his head grinned wildly.

"Jefe. Mire." The group of men at the end of the bar looked up. The man with the gun spat on the floor and the bartender stepped forward to complain, but the Mexican pointed the gun at him and he backed off.

"Jefe." the man called again, keeping his eyes on JT. The group of men parted. Roy sat on a stool, his head tipped back, a shot glass to his lips. He swallowed the whiskey then set the empty glass on the bar and turned. He stared at JT for a moment then burst out laughing.

"Shit. Look what we have here." He grinned. Tobacco stains stood in neat rows in the corners of his teeth. "You remember my friends?"

JT recognized the men at the end of the bar as the Federales he'd met outside Linea. They appeared to have been drinking for a decent amount of time. Several empty shot glasses stood lined up on the bar in front of them.

"Where is she?"

The Mexican who demanded their papers when they met up in the desert lifted his head from the table, grinning wildly, his words slurred. "No es importante." He belched loudly and laid his head back down on the table.

Roy used a fingernail to dislodge a piece of food stuck between his teeth. "Still chasing that half-breed whore?"

JT lurched forward, but two men held him back, each taking hold of one arm.

"Where is she?"

Roy stepped off the stool and faced JT. "It don't appear as how you're in a position to be asking anything." He landed a fist to JT's gut.

"That," Roy said, "is for the Florida Mountains."

JT doubled over, his mouth opening. He lifted his head and stared at Roy.

"Should'a let you hang."

"Shoulda."

Roy hit him again. JT wheezed and a small pool of spit formed on the floor. When he raised his head he spit in Roy's direction and several men moved forward. Roy shooed them away. The gun came out of his holster.

The patrón emerged from the back room. "Fuera," he said to Roy, signaling with a jerk of his head to the door. "No aquí." The patrón's eyes met the bartender's and the bartender reached below the counter.

"Let's you and me take a walk," Roy said, pressing the butt of the barrel against JT's back. "We'll take the back stairs." The men moved to accompany them, but Roy waved them away. "This one's mine, gentlemen." His words were met with laughter and the men returned to their drink. Roy pushed JT forward along a corridor with numbered doors and steered him towards the red door at the end. One of the hall doors opened and two whores and their client stepped into the hallway, moving away when they saw Roy's gun. Roy touched the barrel of the gun to the brim of his hat at the women and motioned JT on.

The red door opened into the back alley JT had seen the woman with the hairpin pass through earlier. Roy pushed him forward again and he fell over a garbage can lying on its side. Broken glass from the remnants of a Jack Daniel's bottle sawed through the fabric of his jeans, slicing into his left knee.

"What the hell's wrong with you?" Roy said.

"Where is she?"

"Shut up. Just shut your goddamn mouth and let me think." JT made to stand, but Roy pushed him back to his knees.

"Goddamn sonofabitch. You can't just let it go."

"Where is she?"

Like a broken record you are. You need to give this up, you hear me?

"I can't."

"Don't give me any of that *can't* shit. You know this ain't going to end good.

"Says the man who's not about harming women."

Roy stopped pacing. "Just what do you expect to do, huh? Stroll in there and pluck her out of a bunch of putas and make your way to the door with no one having any say how?"

"Why not?"

"You shittin' me? You think you can mess with these people like you was asking them to a goddamn dance?"

"I mean to do it."

Roy shook his head. "You're making a mistake cowboy. You got no idea what kind of dangerous you're dealing with. These aint your white livered bottle-suckers in Clayton, boy. You can't come it, not by a long chalk."

"Where is she?"

"Hell, you passed her room on the way out that door."

JT made to stand again, but Roy laid the butt of the revolver on his head and pushed him back down.

"Goddamn it. Goddamn it all to hell. Like a dog with a bone."

"It ain't too late to make it right." JT said.

"The hell it ain't."

"You can make it right."

"No, I can't."

"Don't give me none of that can't shit."

Roy stopped pacing. A thin smile turned up the right corner of his mouth. Then it disappeared. He lifted his hat and wiped his brow with the sleeve of his shirt. He stared at JT's back, noticing the sunburn at the base of his neck.

"You ain't never gonna let this thing rest, are you?

"I already told you, I can't."

JT heard the cock of the gun. He felt the muzzle at the base of his skull. Roy sighed.

"No. I don't suppose you can."

18.

The bullet entered the back of the head and exited the temple, leaving a perfectly round .9 mm hole. A streaked line of red followed. No one took note of the sound, other than the pigeons at the end of the alley that briefly scattered, then returned to their scavenging. Even if the patrons of the bar heard the gunshot, they would know it was Roy taking care of business.

JT felt the spray of blood on his back and the collapse of Roy's dead weight on top of him. He shrugged it off and the body hit the ground. He stared at the body in confused disbelief, before turning to see Lupita's father standing behind him, the barrel of his gun still hot, the smell of gunpowder in the air. JT watched him tuck the gun back into his belt underneath his shirt. The Mexican rolled Roy over with his foot and kicked the body then stepped back, satisfied the man was dead.

"¿Tenías matarlo?

The man looked at JT, an odd expression on his face. "Sí."

"Porqué?"

"Porque es un lobo. Un coyote. Que se alimenta de la miseria de los demás." He told JT that he didn't need to tell him this and would JT rather it was him on his way to hell?

JT looked at the body sprawled on the ground. Roy's hat lay a few feet from him. JT picked it up and put in on the back of Roy's head, covering the bullet wound. He thought about how life shapes you beyond what you can control. *Don't I know it.* And the series of events that destines two men towards a reckoning in the debris of

159

an alleyway with one leaving this earth and the other needing to know why.

Lupita's father watched JT, curious.

"¿Tu amigo?"

"In another lifetime, maybe." JT's voice was tired.

"¿Qué?"

"What? No. He's not my friend."

The man said there was little time. They must hurry. Before the body was discovered.

"¿Papá?

In the corner of the alley stood a young girl shadowed by a dumpster, facing the men. She wavered on her feet. The man nodded at his daughter, and Graciela ran to his side. He told JT they would meet him on the outskirts of Juarez, as planned. "Ten cuidado."

JT said if they did not see him in an hour, they should leave without him.

JT re-entered the Blue Swan through the red door into the corridor. Music drifted from the main room, a soft glow of light making the hallway visible. He counted five doors along the hall, three on his right and two on his left. A man with his arm draped over the shoulders of a woman, holding her breast in one hand and a bottle of beer in the other paid him no attention and disappeared into one of the rooms. Two more men, each accompanied by a girl, were led down the hall and disappeared into rooms as well. JT waited, but no more followed. He stood outside one of the two remaining rooms and listened. Silence. He moved to the second room where heavy grunting sounds filtered through the thinness of the plywood door accompanied by the springs of the box mattress squeaking under the strain of a large man's weight. He returned to the first door, placed his hand on the doorknob and turned, then quietly stepped inside.

The space was dark, filled with the fetid air of a room unaired for too long. He waited. The rhythm of steady breathing reached his ears.

"Dalia?" he whispered in the dark. His fingers reached along the wall for a light switch and flipped it on. The room suddenly lay bathed in a red glow from the draped lamp shades in opposite corners of the room. Above the bed hung a crudely drawn retablo of the Virgin Mary, her arms outstretched in mock supplication. He moved to the side of the bed and stared down at the prone figure sprawled on the mattress. His knees weakened.

She lay clothed in a whore's nightgown, hair knotted and tangled, flowing onto the thin pillow beneath her head. Caked makeup covered her face and rouge stained her cheeks. Thick brick-red lipstick lined her lips, some of it smeared onto her teeth. Both arms were tied to opposite posts of the bed with ragged strips of rope. Dried blood stained the filthy linen sheets where it had cut into her wrists as she struggled. Bruises climbed the length inside her arm, some fresh, some faded. And next to them needle marks. A throbbing began in his head where the gash had healed. He took off his hat and laid it against his chest, tears forming in the corners of his eyes, then he placed it back on his head.

From his left boot he removed a pocket knife, running his hand along its edge to test its sharpness. He bent down and cut the ropes anchoring each of her arms. Then quietly he called her name again. "Dalia." Still asleep her head turned in his direction, then back towards the wall. His hands trembled as he gently smoothed the hair across her forehead. The girl on the bed gave a startled cry and recoiled from his touch, rolling herself into a fetal position, knees tight about her chest. A scream bubbled up, but the hoarseness in her throat made the sound a growl.

"Dalia." He sat on the bed and placed a hand on her arm. She jerked away, her fingers finding his face, raking a trail of clawed scratches down the right side of his neck.

"Dalia." But she rasped louder, a moaning wail that cut to the very core of his soul. She scrambled off the bed and stood crouched in the corner of the room, hissing, and spitting, sniffing the air. He stood, transfixed, not recognizing the girl in front of him; half of him wanting to cry at the inhumanity of the world and the other half filled with undeniable hope that she was alive. He had found her. *She's alive*.

"Dalia, Dalia," he said again. "It's me, JT."

This time his words reached her. She froze and raised her head.

"It's me, JT. ¿El Paraíso Rancho?" He waited. "¿El imbécil?"

She reached out her hand then, uncertain of the space between them, groping the air.

"I'm right here."

Her fingertips reached his face, travelled the length of it until they reached the fabric of his shirt. She rushed towards him, folding into his arms, grasping his shirt until her knuckles turned white. Large gulping sobs wracked her body. He held her and let her cry. Moments passed. He tried to pull her from him so he could talk, but she refused, pushing back against his chest, continuing to weep.

"We have to leave."

She nodded into his chest, still clutching his shirt.

"I'm not going to let you go. I promise. Lo prometo." She nodded again and tried to slow her breathing, now thick from the efforts of crying.

He opened the door to the hall. It was vacant. As he stepped out into the corridor Dalia pulled him back. She had hold of his shirt in a tight grip and he could feel the trembling in her hands.

"Come on, I got you."

She held tight to hand as they made their way to the red door and out into the street.

J T had visions of the young boy disappearing with Ruby. But as he rounded the street he saw both the boy and the horse where he had left them. He reached into his pocket and pulled out a dollar and handed it to the boy, who stared at Dalia.

"Piérdase," JT said. The boy ran off. At the end of the street he looked back at the macabre scene—the young American cowboy, an ugly scar running across his brow and the front of his left pant leg from the knee down soaked in blood, holding to the reins of the horse and next to him the girl in a dirtied and torn nightgown, an obscene trail of blood red lipstick across her mouth and chin, her eyes blackened with the mascara of whores, now dripped into lines of black down her cheeks like the eyes of a circus clown, clinging to the cowboy's side. Then the boy disappeared around the corner. JT swung his leg over Ruby's back while Dalia held onto the saddle's leather. Then he gripped Dalia's hand, held it for a moment so she could feel its strength, and hoisted her up behind him.

"Hold tight," he said. She laid her head against his back and he felt her nod into his shirt.

They met Graciela and her father beyond the outskirts of the city, at the base of the Samalayuca Dunes where they had parted. The father studied Dalia.

"¿Qué pasa?"

JT told the man that she was blind.

He grunted and turned the mule towards the Dunes.

T he Samalayuca dunes bordered the town of Samalyuca, Chihuahua, and lay scattered over the wide expanse of desert to the south. Shaped by the constantly shifting wind in the lee of Cerro de Samalayuca, the medanos towered over the landscape at a couple hundred feet high. A powerful wind buffeted them as they crossed the sand, blowing grit into their eyes and lifting JT's hat. He caught it and pushed it down on his head. He patted Dalia's leg for reassurance and rode on.

They were nearing the base of the dunes when they heard Graciela cry out. Behind them, less than 100 yards away, a group of riders from the bar gave chase.

"Shit." JT said.

"Vamonos," Graciela's father said.

They kicked the flanks of the animals and pushed them forward into a gallop, but the hooves were heavied by the sand. The mule dropped behind, floundering in the sand. Dalia's hands dug into JT, and amid all the chaos, it felt good. He turned his head to see how much ground was gained between them and the Mexicans and was surprised to see them rein up in a neat group. They had stopped. This made him smile until he heard the thunder. JT thought of the night Harlan died and the raging storm that crashed down upon them. He looked to the sky but it came from the earth. Dalia cried out and he turned to the south where he saw the tidal wave of a massive sandstorm. Ruby slowed. He saw that Graciela's father had stopped and was making the sign of a cross across his chest. Ahead of them was the sandstorm, behind them Roy's men.

"We got to ride it out."

"¿Qué?"

"No podemos volver atrás."

The Mexican looked at his daughter, then back at the riders. "¿Cómo?"

JT got down from Ruby and removed the rope on the side of his saddle. He cut a length from it and handed it to Graciela's father.

"Tie it around you both," he said, over the thunder of the sand. He pulled Dalia down from the horse and tied one end of the rope around her waist. He anchored the rope with a couple turns around Ruby's saddle horn, then paid out the other end and tied it to his waist so that they were tethered to the saddle on opposite ends of the rope. He put his lips to Dalia's ear and said, "Sandstorm," then took off his bandana and fashioned it around her neck, pulling it up over her mouth and eyes for protection. He untied his blanket from the back of his saddle and covered Ruby's head. Then he forced the horse down onto her side, her back facing the wind. In the well of her belly he laid Dalia. Before he could join her, the wave overtook him and he was lifted from his feet into white powder.

The posse of riders watched from a safe distance as the sandstorm enveloped the two men and the girls. As it rolled past the spot they had stood, nothing could be seen but white sand, the horizon devoid of all things. The landscape wiped clean.

"Están locos," said one of the riders.

Another one laughed. "Crazy dead." They turned their horses back towards Juarez.

19.

Why do bad things happen Granddad?

There's a balance.

A balance?

Everything has an opposite. Up and down, big and small, dark and light, good and evil. Are you saying we have to have bad to have good?

Sort of. Everything has a dark side.

Why did he do it, Granddad?

Who?

Harlan.

Do what?

Why did Harlan go in after Ruby? Why did he go into that creek?

You know why, JT.

I don't.

He thought you were on that horse.

But I wasn't.

He knows that now.

How come he killed Pa?

Harlan didn't kill your pa.

I saw him.

It wasn't Harlan.

Who was it? Who was it, Granddad?

What's the sense of worrying about that now? It's time you got back to the living boy.

Are you afraid of dying Granddad?

How can I be? I'm already there.

20.

The sun rose into the naked sky, the clouds vanished from the horizon, and buzzards flew circling the mountain pinnacles, the shapes of their outstretched wings shadowed on the ground below. To the south the cordillera stood sentinel in stone columns that stretched deep into the heart of Mexico. In the nights that followed the sandstorm, the moon had risen full and cadaverous, the alabaster light setting off the desert coyotes that yowled in camaraderie at its presence. But the daylight hours stifled heat and flies, an intolerable sun that made even the sturdiest of lizards decline movement beneath its gaze. All traces of wind disappeared and the breezeless air lay heavy and thick to breathe.

Inside the adobe house Lupita held up the five fingers of her right hand. Her mother nodded. Five nights had passed and no sign of her husband or the American. A growing fear had begun to displace hope after the fourth night they had not returned. She thought about this fear, and how she had lived with it all her life, how it sat daily at their table and wondered if this was the way of life and if that was so, why is it something she never grows accustomed to. Death, perhaps can be handled this way, but not fear. It is a disease that eats away with an unflagging hunger. Try as she might, she never felt comfortable in its presence.

She handed Lupita the bucket and watched her disappear through the animal skin covering the door. The hides covering the windows were drawn down. With no breeze, the best they could hope for was a darkened room to lower the heat. She picked up the small straw broom and swept the mud floor like she had every day since she arrived here, not necessarily because the floor needed it, but because doing so made this their home.

"Mamá."

There was an odd quality to Lupita's voice and her mother let the broom drop. She retrieved the revolver hidden in the makeshift altar they constructed to the Virgin Mary. Outside she looked for Lupita who stood alone at the well, the bucket dangling in her hand.

"¿Qué es?"

Lupita pointed. "Mira."

The woman turned her face to the east, her hand rising to shield her eyes from the sun's glare. Shimmering in the distance, coming over the crest of the rise, figures emerged from the sand like golden calves in a dream. Two people on foot and between them one horse. The horse sat two more figures, their hair trailing in the wind.

Dios mío. The words barely uttered and heard over the pounding of her heart. Lupita dropped the bucket and jumped up and down, waving her hand in the air. A wearied hand in the distance raised in salute.

"Prisa," her mother said, "Aqua." She disappeared into the house and placed the gun back in its hiding place. In front of the altar she knelt and made the sign of the cross, making each movement deliberate and sacred across her chest in front of the Virgin Mary. "Gracias bendecido Señora."

Then she went forward to greet her husband and her lost daughter.

E xhausted, dehydrated and numb, they were near collapse when they arrived. They drank the well water Lupita offered, her mother cautioning "beber despacio," lest they swallow too fast and throw up what they consumed. Too fatigued to remain standing they collapsed inside the house, dusty, sandy in all their regalia and she left them there. They slept the sleep of the dead.

It was not until the next day that JT recounted their story. The sandstorm overtook them quickly, and before he could lay down beside Dalia, he was swept up into the eye. Were it not for the rope anchored to his waist he doubted he would be alive. He remembered floating for what seemed a very long time, as though the laws of the universe were suspended and gravity expired. He was a young child again, talking to his grandfather. Then the wind disappeared and he fell hard into the earth and was swallowed. When he awoke, half-buried in sand, he was dazed but unhurt. The sandstorm had moved on, chasing the land to the east and cloaking all in its path. He was alone. He called Dalia's name. Then he remembered the rope tethered to his waist. He pulled on it and it sprang from the ground like a great vine, its length disappearing into the mounded sand. His muscles trembling he continued to tug at the rope until the fabric of her nightgown emerged, and with one last pull he lifted her from the sand. And with her, Ruby lifted her head and rose from the dead.

The sandstorm took the mule. It served its purpose as a windbreak for Graciela and her father, but the animal was old and could not weather the strain of being buried alive. There was nothing could be done for it he told Lupita as she cried. She had a particular fondness for the mule as it was on this animal that her brother delivered her from Juárez.

Dalia's eyesight was poor but improving daily. It was Graciela who told them about the eyedrops, a fix used by the chulos to control the whores. She explained that the blindness was temporary but that it could last for many hours. How many hours she could not say. Sometimes girls were given these drops continuously so that they were kept in blindness for long periods of time, until they were made to yield. Until they were broken.

Graciela spoke with a tremor in her voice, a stutter that her father said was not there before. Her right arm had a unnatural bend to it and she explained that it had been broken and not healed well. At night she dreamed fitful dreams that caused her to twitch and cry out many times in her sleep. It seemed to JT that she lived in a constant state of readiness, a terror that accompanied her at all times. She constantly checked their retreat, fearful of followers. Even after coming in sight of her home. Or maybe especially so. When she first saw the adobe house in the distance she would not believe it was real, so convinced was she that a mirage had sprung up in the desert whose purpose was to deceive and break her heart. So afraid was she of breaking into a thousand pieces if it was not real. As much as she longed to be home, she was frightened of what it meant to be there.

A soft breeze and the smell of cocoa woke him many hours into the second day. A wash of déjà vu came over him so strong he touched his forehead, feeling the healed scar above his left eyebrow. Lupita's mother had given both the girls a strong brew to settle their nerves and bring about a calming sleep. Curled into the bend of his body lay Dalia, in a simple cotton gown given to her by Lupita. Her head was pressed against his chest, her arms tucked close to her chest and her hands balled into little fists beneath her chin. Lucent skin revealed small veins in the corners of her eyelids. So beautiful, so fragile. He smiled, remembering their first meeting and the spark of fire that ignited both her temper and his heart. The caked makeup washed away, the rouge removed from her cheeks and lips, she looked once again like the young girl he spoke with in the corral of her father's ranch weeks ago. Only now he worried that the bruising of her body would etch indelible lines into her heart, to what extent he did not know. The thought of this made him ache, and he chose not to think of it and instead lay back and concentrated on the rhythm of her breathing. Music to his soul. He wanted to capture this moment, imprint this space of time in his mind and pretend all was right in the world, nothing had changed. Because he knew that when he woke, he would leave this room and walk through a door there was no returning to. He could see what he left on the other side of the door, but never again touch it. The truth was he knew this all along. The moment he stepped across the border into the mesa of the Chihuahuan desert. It was a letting go. Laying to rest the past. But also a holding on. Holding on to the promise of a new beginning. It was the time before the dying that mattered. He closed his eyes and slept.

After a time he gently moved his body from her sleeping form and stood. In the inner room Graciela lay asleep on a cot, and in the corner before the altar of the Virgin Mary knelt Graciela's father. His eyes closed and head bent in prayer. JT stepped out into the noonday sun and stretched, the muscles across his back stiff. It was a good kind of pain. He made his way to the back of the house and relieved himself in the brush and when he was finished he walked out amongst the creosote and scrub and stood for a long time gazing at the horizon, thanking whoever was responsible for this impossible day and all the ones to follow.

At the well he found Lupita's mother, beating the dust from the clothes on the stone before she scrubbed them in a tub of water at her feet then left them on the stones to dry.

"Buenos dias."

The woman nodded.

"Me sorprendido que fue."

"¿Por qué?"

She explained that she was surprised her husband had gone to Juarez because he had long mourned Graciela's death. That he believed her return was a rising from the dead, and who's to say what Lazarus was like when he returned to the living. He believes that the dead walk among us, and for them life is a curse. He questions the mercy of showing her what once was, which she cannot be again.

JT remembered the man's talk ... *it contaminates all you touch* ...

He drew the water from the well and drank from the bucket, then poured the remainder over his head, feeling the grit still trapped in his hair slide down his face. Then, in that clear morning of that impossible day, a gunshot rang out. It came from the house.

The bucket clanked against stone as it dropped from JT's hands. He ran towards the house, a cold fear blossoming inside his chest. He tore back the hide covering the door and found Graciela in the front room on the cot, a dead blankness to her eyes. Blood came from a bullet hole in her right temple. As he stood staring at her another shot rang out.

"No." He rushed into Dalia's room and there on the floor with blood spreading out around him, lay Lupita's father. In his hand, the gun JT had seen in Juárez. JT's eyes travelled from him to Lupita, who stood above her father, the revolver taken from the makeshift altar still warm in her hands. His eyes went to Dalia lying on the pallet on the floor in the corner of the room in the same position he had left her.

"Dalia...?"

"No." Lupita said, "No se lo permitiría."

JT looked at the man again, his body slack, a halo of bright red stretched across the floor, blood reaching into the pebbled holes in the dirt floor scratched by the chickens. He became aware the man's wife was standing next to him, the lines on her face cut hard like they had been made with a knife, a look of horror on her face. Her trembling hand raised to cover her mouth. Tears wet her eyes and she reached out her other hand to touch Lupita. As she did so the revolver dropped from Lupita's hand and she fell on her knees beside it, not lifting her gaze from the dead man on the ground.

"Lupita?" JT said.

"No es verdad."

"What is not true?"

She spoke in an impassive voice and continued to stare at her father. She told JT that the things that happened, the things they suffered, the things Graciela and Dalia suffered, these were terrible things, done by terrible people. "Vivo con esto aqui." She pressed a hand to her chest. She did not want these memories in her heart, but in her heart is where they live. These terrible things changed them, made them different. She paused and looked down at her father. She said that this was not the only truth of how they are different. Every day they are made to remember in the eyes of the ones they love. The ones who love them, who say they love them, who beg them not to be changed. It lives in their eyes. "Sus ojos tristes." They do not mean to, but they cannot stop. They cannot help but you see this way, no matter how hard they try. Their eyes say you are damaged and will never be whole again. Every day she is reminded by these eyes what is lost to them. Not what is saved. What is lost. "Y nos recuerdan."

... you have the child, but you have lost the child ...

Her mother knelt beside her and smoothed Lupita's hair as she spoke. Tears flowed freely down the girl's cheeks. She buried her head into her mother's embrace and sobbed. Her mother raised her head to look at JT and continued to speak for her daughter.

She told JT that the family does not want to feel this way, they hate themselves for feeling this way. But that does not change the truth that they do. And soon the child comes to believe that the ones she loves are themselves forever changed. Because of the child. The child believes she has damaged them.

Lupita cried harder, nodding into her mother's chest. Her mother continued. It is another paradox. ¿Lo ves? You return to a place you knew as sanctuary only to find that it has become a prison. Not just for you, but for them too. And now the child makes room in their heart to carry this burden as well. Believing that being alive has forever changed the people they love. Changed their lives in an irreparable way. A terrible irreparable sin.

... simply a different kind of death ...

Lupita raised her head from her mother's breast and spoke. "Mi padre pensaba que nos estaba poniendo fuera de nuestra miseria. Pero la verdad es que nos estaba poniendo fuera de su." She told JT that her father would like to believe he was putting them out of their misery. But the truth is ... he was putting them out of his. Then she broke from her mother's embrace and lay down beside her father and refused to move.

JT's hands shook as he picked Dalia up in his arms and carried her from the house. In the lean-to he sat down in the straw with her cradled her in his arms and wept. A wave of grief swelled up in him so sudden, so strong it scared him. For Ma, for Granddad, for Harlan. Mostly Harlan. Somehow he knew that voice in his head was gone forever. It wasn't coming back. A part of him would always look for it, grieve for it. But in his arms lay the flesh and blood of his life and his future. He kissed the warmth of her forehead, then finally gave into relief and let the gnawing fear inside himself go.

EPILOGUE

Dear Dalia,

Come back to me.

I see the dullness in your eyes and the way my reflection lays flat against them with no remembering. How you refuse to let any light in. And it scares me because I can't see the anger behind it. The spunk that drives you. I know you can hear me; I know you're in there; it's in the way your hands dig into me when we're riding like you're hanging on for dear life, afraid you're gonna fall. But here's what I need you to know: It's okay to fall. Go ahead ... fall into me. God as my witness, I promise I'll catch you. I will.

Do you recall what a jackass I was the first time we met? You were too busy cussing me out to notice I couldn't keep my eyes from you. You sure as hell wanted me to know that the sun don't come up just so I can hear myself crow. There was fire in you girl; pure passion spilling out. And I was so taken in by the power of it, the strength of it, I hardly paid attention that it was directed at me. You weren't fixing to let no man, no how, see his way to changing you. And I knew right then and there I needed to see you again; knew that the whole of my existence was just preparing me for you.

I never told anybody this, but losing my brother was the hardest thing I thought I'd ever have to live through. There was something about this deal he and I made with life and against Pa that if we got through growing up and stepped into boots, we'd walk through living the rest of it together. We'd be able to handle what the world threw at us cause we had survived the worst. And we had each other. So his leaving hit me hard, real hard. Partly because I didn't see it coming. But mostly because I felt cheated. Cheated out of belonging somewhere and not having to go it alone. The days after he left were god-awful slow and I let them drift by one by one in a string of nothingness until they

179

amounted to little more than time I was marking 'til I got to join him. I couldn't see the point in making something out of a life that kicked you down every time you got up. Until one night out on the prairie Harlan came to me in my dreams and told me to wake up. He said I couldn't hang my future on something I thought life owed me cause it don't work that way. Life don't make no deals, he said, and even if we do all that we think is asked of us, that don't mean we're gonna be saved—in this life or the next. And if I couldn't get that straight, it didn't matter where I stood— between heaven and hell—I'd still be in hell and only a fool would choose that. And did I want to spend the rest of my time on earth in a place where all the meanness in the world sinks to? He said it was letting Pa win. And I knew it.

I'm telling you this because I've been where you are now—that place between heaven and hell—and I know that all you can see is the unfairness of what life's dealt you. And I'm not going to tell you you're wrong, or that it don't exist, or that it won't be waiting for you when you come back. Cause it will. I imagine there are things you can't talk about now; things you can't talk about ever. I know it. I won't ask you. I'll wait 'til you're ready. And if that day never comes, that'll be okay too. But it's the giving up, the surrendering that's got me worried. It's not like you, girl, to go down without a fight and let them claim victory. You're strong. We're strong. You don't have to go this alone. And while losing Harlan brought me to the very edge of dying, losing you would surely kill me. I swear it would. Cause I ain't planning on being anywhere that you're not at.

I won't never give up on you girl. Ever. That's a promise.

Come back to me.

I love you,

JT

GRATITUDE

Thank you to Shipwreckt Books, Tom Driscoll and his wife Beth Stanford; Abigail DeWitt; Dawn Shamp, Table Rock Writers Workshop in Little Switzerland, North Carolina, (Georgann, Donna, Cindy—you know who you are); Kim and Patricia Chesser, Burnt Well Ranch in Roswell, New Mexico; Dave McIntosh Eric Finkelstein; Starry Night Retreat Residency Program in Truth or Consequences, New Mexico; my professors and peers at UMKC; my writing groups; The Writer's Place, Kansas City, Missouri, Duchesne Clinic in Kansas City, Kansas; Saint Vincent Clinic in Leavenworth, Kansas; family, friends and many more. And special thanks to my boys who never wavered in their encouragement, always believing I was the engine that could.

ABOUT THE AUTHOR

Anne Muccino lives in Kansas City where she completed her B.A. in English, Creative Writing at UMKC. Her short stories, essays and poems have been published in *Kansas City Voices, Literary Laundry, Rusty Truck, Number One Magazine, Work Stew, Lost Lake Folk Opera* and others. *Red Bricks* is her debut novel.